SALT

a novel

Danielle Boursiquot

Empty Hands
New York

Danielle Boursiquot/Empty Hands Media, LLC
Forest Hills, NY 11375
www.danielleboursiquot.com

Publisher's Note: This is a work of fiction. Names, characters, places, and incidents are a product of the author's imagination. Locales and public names are sometimes used for atmospheric purposes. Any resemblance to actual people, living or dead, or to businesses, companies, events, institutions, or locales is completely coincidental.

Ordering Information:
Quantity sales. Special discounts are available on quantity purchases by corporations, associations, and others. For details, contact the "Special Sales Department" at the address above.

SALT/ Danielle Boursiquot. -- 1st ed.
ISBN 978-0-9980697-0-8
Library of Congress Control Number: 2016920389

"But if you tame me, then we shall need each other. To me you will be unique in all the world. To you, I shall be unique in all the world."

-Antoine de Saint-Exupéry, The Little Prince

For the girls. All you who have tamed me.

With all thine offerings, thou shalt offer salt.

—Leviticus 2:13

1 Cloak and Dagger

I was stealing moments to talk to you because I was afraid that every chance could have been our last. There were eyes peeking around every inch of this place and ears tuned in to the smallest of sounds, like the floorboards creaking, blinds being pulled up, even the goddamned toilet flushing. We were definitely being watched.

It was a lot of work staying one step ahead of everybody, and I'll admit you weren't making things easy. I was moving slower and slower and it didn't take much for me to break into a sweat at a certain point. They thought they had me hemmed in, for my own sake of course. Every little need was tended to, from the extra soft toilet paper to the smoothies I liked being made fresh every morning. They kept their eyes peeled for my changing moods, but they forgot that Carly made me a master of disguise a long time ago. I mean, I was handling glitter powder and greasy rouge when I was still learning how to read at P.S. 189. After school, instead of getting started on homework, I dabbed white highlight and kohl shadow on my face to practice either the villain, or the damsel in distress in the bathroom mirror. When Carly performed, I always had access to backstage doorways and stairwells where I could study different ways to throw someone off my scent. I practiced folding my hands in my lap with shoulders hunched, bringing my chin to my chest for praying, giggling with squinted eyes to show how funny the joke I didn't even hear was, or opening my eyes wide to take in every bit of light and never blinking to show how seriously I was taking whatever the adult in the room was saying. It's a thin line between deceiving and acting, I know, but we don't have time to debate those finer points now. I couldn't let them catch me before I was ready to be caught. I was telling on them too, after all.

I crept around this house like an intruder, even though they were definitely the ones intruding. Our people came and went on a weekly rotation from Jersey, Michigan, Québec, and Miami. The Wolf's three brothers brought their women and at least two children apiece, pretty much camping out all over the house. Now, keep in mind that our brownstone has three floors so there's room enough for everybody to spread out and be comfortable like normal people. There's guest rooms, a pullout sofa in the ground floor parlor and even a huge leather futon and a flat screen television in the basement. Extra bathrooms, too. But they all insisted on cramming into one room every night until real late, whispering about the situation and what's to be done about us. I was a prisoner dragging a bunch of balls and chains everywhere, but it was all right. I knew my jailers, and I even loved them. When they heard, they came like magi; some carrying stories from the old days, others carrying prayers for the days to come, and empty hands to lay on me every chance they got. They'll have their versions for you and I know they'll all mean well, but they don't know everything. No matter what they say about themselves, or about me, there's things only I can tell.

Like, I never did enjoy red lipstick. That was more of a Ziz thing. She wore it every day, even though our math teacher, Madame Busioc, made her take it off as soon as she spotted her trying to hide in the back of the class. *"Mademoiselle, enlevez-moi ça tout de suite!"* She marched over to her with the box of tissues from the front desk and waited for her to wipe it all off. It was ridiculous because Ziz kept a tube of Wet-n-Wild in the pocket of her uniform blazer ready to reapply in the locker room as soon as class was over. She came back with the same angry mouth day after day, the same routine. Our geography teacher with the orthopedic shoes and torpedo boobs, Madame LaFalaise, would just squint and shake her head. The hunky monitor that all the girls giggled about, Monsieur Mellul, would roll his eyes and huff as he stomped past us down the hall, but my best friend had no regard.

One time a bunch of us went to the mall after school and I ended up stealing an expensive tube of lipstick. I didn't take it on purpose, I swear. I had on this gigantic pink coat with wide cushioned pockets that looked like buckets attached to my sides. We trotted in, smiling at the security guards who gritted their teeth whenever they saw teenagers crawling through the aisles. We went straight for the main floor and stopped at all the perfume and makeup counters. Dominique and Geneviève pulled their hair back and hung costume jewelry earrings up to their cheeks. Corrine asked a clerk to measure her ring size. While I stood next to Maria watching her spritz herself with one of the men's colognes because it reminded her of Mellul, Ziz leaned against me and said that we were going to be late.

"Late for what?"

The saleswoman looked at us and kept going back and forth like she couldn't tell the difference between our two faces. Aziza bugged her eyes open wide and looked in the direction of the security guard by the revolving doors. I wasn't getting it, so she grabbed my arm and started running for the exit, leaving the other girls behind. When we had cleared the Metro turnstiles and were standing on the down escalator she turned to me, breathless with excitement.

"Come on, gimme!"

"Give you what?"

She pointed at my pocket, "The lipstick you just boosted!"

"What? What are you talking about?" I reached in and pulled out a black lacquer tube with a gold band around the middle. Wide-eyed, I turned it around in my hand like a jewel. Ziz grabbed it from me and howled with laughter.

"You're a criminal now, baby! *Yahaaa!*"

What's crazy is that I still buy that lipstick. I might have only worn it on four or five occasions in the last twenty years, but I could never let my makeup box be without a fresh tube. Especially now. For our clandestine meetings, I always reached for my tube of Matador Red. I put on fringe-y Zanotti sandals or some Chanel riding boots, depending on how far I was walking. I wrapped my head with some fabulous Nigerian fabric and wore dark sunglasses. I'd say I was going to the library, or to the nail salon, or maybe to the restaurant to check up on things. I'd put on a billowing trench coat with the collar gathered around my neck and clip on simple gold earrings. I get that the whole diva-in-hiding act probably did more to attract attention than to camouflage me. I know. But those days called for special drama, and dammit, you were going to learn from the best.

Sometimes the tension in the house would get really thick and God bless him, the Wolf stayed cool. He always knew when I couldn't breathe and made sure we had our space without ever having to show his fangs. Sometimes a low growl was necessary when the jailers tried too hard to be helpful, but it never went beyond that. I went to see movies that I knew damn well no one else would want to see. That was a sure-fire tactic. Something with talking trees, or foreign with a dreamy Italian lead saying dramatic things like, '*non sarò mai d'accordo con te. Mai!'* I'd get up early and slip out of the house before anyone had a chance to offer me a lift or a charity come-with, and I'd wait for you on a bench in Prospect Park with a notebook or a gossip rag. I never cared where some pop star went on vacation or how honored some actor was to have received yet another award. I'd just turn the pages until you were ready to listen.

On our park bench, I crossed my legs at the ankle and positioned my foot so that the heel on my four-hundred-dollar sling-backs caught the light. That's right, I posed. When you meet my grandmother Hélène, you'll understand what I'm talking about. I'd watch the cool Brooklyn bohos go by with their toddlers and I'd wonder if they could tell what we're doing out there in the mid-morning. I wonder if they noticed us at all.

If the weather didn't allow for the park, I'd take a cab into the city and sometimes end up at Bloomingdale's. I could stay anonymous in those careless crowds of tourists and snotty locals, letting my fingertips slide along the glass displays. At this point, the model types poised with perfume bottles and cardboard swatches didn't approach me. They stood back and let me sniff and browse on my own. Maybe they thought I was some expensive lady being incognito and watched quietly as I slipped between their bursts of amber, and lily, and rose. I'd take the escalator and leave them behind so I could shuffle between the designer racks undisturbed.

Sometimes I'd end up at a Lower East Side hole in the wall where the menus were taped to the tables under bottles of ketchup and hot sauce. It was easy to hide from prying eyes there. The delivery guy with frayed jeans and dirty hoodie wheeling in cases of soda didn't care about my note scribbling. His sleeves were pushed up to his elbows to expose pale hairless arms. It wasn't the kind of place with table service, but after a quick once over the cashier was compelled to bring me my plastic tray loaded with a drippy cheese steak sandwich, bag of salt and vinegar chips, and lemonade. The Wolf would've had a fit if he saw me eat that crap. He was my main jailer, but in spite of everything he did let me out for good behavior because he knew what it was between us. He understood what it had to be.

Other times I got crafty and hid in plain sight at the Junior's on DeKalb. It was a real bold move for me to sit right at the counter to order cause they knew how much I loved a good slice of strawberry cheesecake. And they knew I wouldn't go to just any crappy place where the cake is all mushy with no taste and the glaze is just some chewy gelatin with food coloring. When I'd get my giant slice, I'd admire it for a moment, and then start carving out tiny bites with my fork until only the strawberries were left. I ate those whole.

It was kind of funny to be dodging eyes trying to monitor my every move, every bead of perspiration, and every heavy sigh. In spite of everything I'd already been through, it seems I'd suddenly become fragile. At home, all I had to do was clear my throat, and there were five annoyingly well-meaning hands handing me a glass of water or trying to check my pulse, repeating some doctor's instructions I didn't want to hear about. They didn't understand that this was just between us. They would have tried to interfere, put in their two cents everywhere and get all involved. That was just out of the question.

DANIELLE BOURSIQUOT

2 Impératrice

Margo Impératrice arrived at her daughter's home one morning in spring and started counting days. As she walked up the cobblestone path, birds lifted from the banana trees. In the breeze, their wide leaves sent down leftover spray from the early rain, and it fell like whispers. The roosters had long since stopped crowing, but in the house, Hélène sat at the kitchen table in her silk robe staring down at her slippers. The morning pot of coffee was hot on the tray in front of her, but her cup was still empty. The cook had tried to fill it, but Hélène waved her off and just sat there with her arms folded, bracing for something. The sudden knock at the door woke her from her daze and she adjusted her belt to go peek at who it was. At the vestibule, she was rattled to find that it was her mother's tall shadow leaning long across the porch. Margo stood motionless until her daughter opened the door to let her in.

"Oh, *Manman*, you didn't tell me you were coming!"

Margo gave a sober nod and stepped in.

"How did you come, *Manman*? Did someone drive you here? Do you have bags?"

"I left my things with your guardian at the gates. Don't worry."

"Oh. OK, come. Come in."

The driver had already taken the girls to school and the servants were out of sight. The breakfast dishes were washed, and the whole first floor had been swept and mopped, but the smell of fresh cinnamon porridge and coffee still hung in the air. The pillows on the parlor sofa were lined up by size and color. There was a vase of cut roses in each room next to family portraits and positioned next to little trays of pot-pourri. The French doors to the gingerbread patio were open, with lace curtains lifting in the breeze, but there was disarray in the quiet of that morning.

Margo had never been to her daughter's home in
Pacot, but it was just as she had expected. There
were two floors joined by a curved staircase. The
bedrooms, a full bath, and patio were upstairs, and
the parlor, powder room, formal living room and
dining room were downstairs with the servant
quarters connected to the kitchen in the back. She
made her way down the main hall until she came to
the informal dining space. Hélène followed as her
mother looked around. The dinette and cabinets
were painted pale yellow. The armoire was neatly
stacked with the every day plates and plain cups.
She ran her hand over the butcher-block counter
and looked out the window at the cook preparing
the pots and pans for lunch. The white Frigidaire in
the corner gave a constant low hum. Margo took
her pipe from a fold in her head wrap and rolled it
between her fingers. She aimed her gaze at her
daughter, standing quietly with her hands fidgeting
in front of her.

Hélène avoided her mother's eyes. She still felt
like a child waiting for permission to speak, even
though she was a wife and the mother of three
daughters. She volunteered at church teaching the
children of house servants to read and write, and
she regularly worked in her own lush garden
clipping stems and pulling weeds. She preferred

tending to her plants and flowers to socializing with the matrons and other young wives who spent their days shopping and gossiping about other people. They went around smiling with their eyeballs running over each others' hair and clothes nitpicking every little thing, but they were the military wives and widows she at least occasionally had to mingle with because of who she was married to.

There was a yard man on staff, but she enjoyed puttering around the roses she had along both sides of the house herself. She had ordered bushes of Love's Promise from a nursery in New York and cared for them like fragile children. Even after Marie Lourdes was born, she pruned and watered them in a careful routine and kept the beds picture perfect. When Marie Madeleine came, she struggled to find time for her roses and they lost their pristine presentation. Brush flowers and plants grew wild in the hills beyond the property, and the ever-present Bougainvillea crept up in messy patches on all sides. Just after Mathilda was born, bunches of *Honteuse* started filling in every other clear inch, competing with the roses for space.

Hélène allowed only French to be spoken in the house and chastised the girls when she caught them braying with their classmates or neighborhood children in Kréyol. They had all three received, at one time or another, a wooden spoon across their knuckles for saying *pouki sa* instead of *pourquoi,* or for sucking their teeth in frustration like the cook did all the time. Mimose, the nanny and housekeeper was only a few years younger than Hélène, but she enforced her mistress' rules to the letter, except when she slipped little wax paper packages of peanut brittle between the girls' pillows, or gave them an extra piece of *dous makos* after dinner.

Hélène was a beautiful woman, but had never developed the confidence to go with it. As a girl, she'd been spared the bouts of acne her classmates suffered almost all at the same time. Her velvety tone always made other girls jealous. While they scrubbed their cheeks with grainy pastes and smeared on layers of Vénus de Milo, Hélène got away with using a washcloth and cold water and it left her with milk chocolate skin. Along with everything else their neighbors whispered about Margo, the word was that she was also a *mambo* who worked some *wanga* to make her daughter the most beautiful girl in the neighborhood. Now, her beautiful daughter had puffy circles under her eyes and dark marks along her temple and jaw. Her bottom lip was discolored in the middle from constant gnawing at the tender flesh until it bled. She walked with her head at a perpetual tilt and with her shoulders squared back like a pageant girl. She was careful to project only the most pleasing disposition, in every situation, in every room, as though at any moment a host with slick hair and brilliant teeth would appear with a microphone to ask for her thoughts on the most appropriate dishes for a dinner party, or her opinion on wearing a hat versus a mantilla in church.

Every morning, especially when her husband was home, she inspected her face in the bathroom mirror for the best makeup strategy. Soft Cocoa was closer to her skin tone, but Warm Caramel covered bruises much better. She had rehearsed the outside smile that she used to cover the inside hurts for so many years that it was as automatic as flipping a light switch. The morning her mother arrived, though, every bulb was blown out and the outside smile wouldn't come. Margo wedged the neck of her pipe between her jaws and lifted her daughter's chin to examine her bare face. She traced her hard fingers from forehead to chin and from ear to ear. Hélène closed her eyes and let her arms go limp.

Margo looked over her daughter's face like a map and saw places she never knew were there. After a long silence, Margo said simply, "One hundred." Hélène opened her eyes and wordlessly asked what that meant, knowing she would not get an answer.

❧

"Papa's coming home today!"

"Mathilda, be quiet! You're always screaming!"

"Girls, your grandmother is sleeping! Mimose! Come do something with them!"

"*Oui, Madame.*"

Hélène tiptoed quickly from room to room adjusting already arranged pillows, shifting perfectly placed picture frames a millimeter over and back again, open and closing drawers, and checking the setting on the oscillating fan near the front door. When Mimose finally shepherded the girls to their bedrooms, Hélène took a moment to sit on the edge of the sofa with her knees together and her back straight. She put her palm to her chest, closed her eyes and waited for her breath and heartbeat to get back to speaking terms before she stood up again. She walked slowly to the record player and put on one of her Dalida albums at low volume. She was wearing a yellow linen dress with capped sleeves and a matching wide belt from Chez Lalouche in Port-au- Prince. That shop carried luxury designs along with accessories like hats and scarves and purses. She usually came home with some new piece that she knew the heavy matrons wouldn't be able to squeeze themselves into, no matter how strong the girdle or skilled the tailor. Her yellow dress that day was a clean and simple style. It was more like what the Americans, like Jackie Kennedy, were wearing. Hélène loved the First Lady's look and tried to mimic it right down to the short white gloves and pillbox hat. She slipped her feet into beige kitten heels and set her make up case in front of the mirror. Her nails were already painted in Peach Shimmer and her straightened hair was neatly curled under, barely grazing her short strand of pearls. She looked at herself in the mirror and imagined that Dalida's sultry voice, dipping and rising in her haunting tremolo, was like a piece of clothing or a layer of makeup that would give her the effect she wanted for that day: an irresistible prize to come home to. Her heart drummed with anticipation, in rhythm with the music. She swept Soft Coral onto her eyelids and traced black pencil along the lash line into a cat eye. She brushed a fine dusting of Warm Peach onto the apples of her cheeks and smoothed Kiss of Honey on her lips for a finishing touch. When she finally heard the truck lumber up the driveway and the heavy clang of the

driver's door, she put on her most welcoming smile
and ran to lower the music. Her mind raced for an
explanation and she felt her feet start sweating
inside her shoes.

As soon as Edgar stepped in, Hélène rushed to
wrap her arms around him with the confidence of a
young girl wearing a grown woman's perfume. She
stretched up onto her toes and clung to him so the
lilac spray on her neck would take over any other
smell he might have brought with him from the
capital. Gasoline and metal from the open truck,
fried goat and plantains bought from a *machann* on
the roadside, sweat soaked into the cotton of his
khaki uniform, cheap perfume from some cheap
thing leaning on her elbows at a novelty shop selling
old pain-killers, plastic shower caps, and frying
pans. There was always some cheap thing waiting in
the dust along his path, but they never made it to
the house. Their scent was the only part of them
that could ever cross her gates. That was the
unspoken rule. When she pulled away, she took his
hat and stepped back, almost posing.

"Welcome home, *mon amour.*"

"*Merci.*"

With just one word Edgar's baritone filled the
room. It was more than his broad chest, the tight
set of his full lips, or the heavy gun belt around his

waist. He moved decisively and didn't waste his gestures. With only a squint of his dark eyes or the lift of his palm, he could cause thunder and lightning to boom and crack within the walls of his house and in every chamber of his wife's heart. He looked into the dining room, and before Hélène could speak, he stopped, staring at the six place settings at the table where there were usually five. He turned slowly to her.

"My mother is visiting. She came yesterday."
There was a slight undulation on the left side of his jaw. An almost imperceptible twitch that would have been missed by anyone else, but Hélène knew all the invisible shifts in Edgar's body and used them as a roadmap. She knew the sigh that meant she should stand behind his chair and press her soft fingers into his shoulders. She knew the wrinkle in his forehead that meant the girls were making too much noise and that Mimose needed to quiet them down. She knew the squaring of his back that meant she should melt into the walls and make no sound at all. There was only a fifty percent chance that she could distract Edgar with her girlish smile or soothe him with the scent between her breasts, but before she had a chance to lean into him again, he turned and went upstairs to shower and change.

At supper, Edgar sat at the head of the table and Margo sat at the foot. In the heavy silence, every word was weighed and measured.

"Seigneur, pour votre bonté divine, nous vous remercions et nous soumettons à votre gré. Amen."

A simple request for salt here, an offering of water there. Every scrape of a fork cut through the thickness in the room. The girls were still young, but as military daughters they knew enough to use their mouths only for eating at the table. They controlled their urge to jabber and stayed quiet unless they were spoken to first.

"Is everything good at school?"

"Yes, Papa."

"Yes, Papa."

"Yes, Papa."

"Good."

The evening air in the hills was usually cool, but perspiration gathered behind Hélène's neck and caused her hairline to frizz.

"The food is good."

"Yes. Do you want more sauce?"

"No, thank you. I'm fine."

A random cough, or loud swallow of water made everyone's eyes shift from Margo's face to Edgar's to see where the sparks would fly from first. But nothing happened. The cook kept her head down as she shuffled in to clear the empty plates.

After supper, it was Handel's *Messiah* on the record player. Edgar sat in his wingback chair with a glass of rum and a copy of *Les Fleurs du Mal* in his lap. On the sofa, Hélène busied her hands with some flowery needlepoint. Margo placed herself strategically between them in a stiff-backed chair with her cold pipe cradled in her hand as the genteel charade began. At the crack of a match, Hélène looked toward Edgar for a sign of displeasure. She tried to pinpoint the flinch of his jaw or the purse of his lips, but there was nothing. As irritated as Edgar may have been, Hélène knew he would never engage Margo in an argument. A military man always knew how to keep a stone expression while breathing gasoline fumes, during the beating of a folk singer with too many hot words for the president, even in the face of a staunch old woman with sparks in her eyes.

After quick deliberate drags, Margo exhaled a first lungful of sweet smoke into the air. Hélène crossed and uncrossed her ankles but could not get comfortable as she watched her mother blow out the match and extinguish the hot tip with her tongue. Edgar continued reading, making no move other than to ceremoniously turn each page. The music could not distract from the paper rustling, the teeth clicking against the pipe, the smoke hovering high above them like a ghostly mist settling into their skin. After a while, Hélène rose to open a window. The ceiling fan above them whirred steadily, but it wasn't enough to diffuse the thickening air. She gave her husband another quick glance, but there was no change in his countenance. She sat back down to continue her work.

"Are you all right?"

His voice broke the silence and startled her. He had not even looked up.

"Oh yes, darling" she said. "I'm fine. Thank you."

Margo tapped her fingers against her pipe as she dragged in and breathed out. Every now and then there was a burst of laughter from upstairs, followed by Mimose hushing the girls. After what felt like hours, Edgar finally closed his book and rose. He walked over to his wife and kissed her on the forehead.

"*Bonne nuit*," he said.

"I'll be there right after I check on the girls," Hélène said, looking up, waiting for his approval. He gave it with a gentle touch on her cheek, but his hand fell away before she had time to feel its warmth.

Edgar nodded dutifully to his mother-in-law. "Impératrice."

"Colonel." She nodded back.

They addressed each other by title. The only difference was that Margo was born with hers. They had been groomed on very different fields and Edgar's hands had taken several lives already, while Margo's were still clean. Technically. But they were rivals from the day they met, and they still competed for power. She had allowed him to take her daughter without resistance and accepted everyone's congratulations with quiet grace. Which of those country girls would've turned down a handsome young officer in crisp khaki offering a title and the promise of white-glove living in Port-au-Prince? But the dry letters that came every few months from her daughter, those letters in smooth penmanship that described balls at the National Palace and round the clock electricity, lost teeth, good report cards, or the roses on the grounds of the new house growing larger and more fragrant with each passing season did not fool her for a moment.

Margo was fourteen when her parents died in a flood. The local nuns sent her to Port-au-Prince to be a housemaid for a French family for room and board. The nuns would visit once a month to check on her, to make sure the family was pleased with her service. Within three months their nineteen year old son, a blond waif with a constant snarl to his top lip even when he smiled, had tried a number of times to touch Margo in a way that she didn't welcome. His touching seemed almost an afterthought when he waited for his parents to retire to their room after supper. He'd linger in the kitchen while Margo piled the dishes and flatware in a wide bucket to take outside for washing and wait for her to start shuffling under the weight of the bucket to come press himself against her from behind. The first time he did it, she froze and almost dropped all the plates. He looked away as he groped her small breasts and rubbed his groin on her. Margo did her best to stand perfectly still until he was done and walked on without looking back at that snarl he probably still had while he slept.

It was a matter of time before he starting creeping into her small room off the kitchen at night to climb on top of her and rub himself on her, not through her cotton and his cotton, but skin to skin, something rougher and faster and sweaty, without having to look at her face. He was afraid of himself, that much she could tell. He wanted things that were not available to him, things he had to seek out and keep secret. She was tall and hard, but quiet. It was easy and his right to do what he wanted with her while imagining what he really desired.

The night before she left that home, the blond waif had come into Margo's room very late. She had barely drifted to sleep when the curtain separating her bed from the rest of the tiny room lifted. She turned onto her back and for the first time looked at him full in the face. In the moonlight, his snarl looked softer and his hair fell into his eyes. He was so slight that his broad shoulders curved forward and made him look nervous. Margo stayed still and watched the rise and fall of the thin nightshirt against his chest. He lifted his bare foot and pressed it gently onto Margo's chest. He touched the wall for balance and traced his toes from between her breasts, down to her belly, to rest over her warm pubis. She thought about screaming. She thought about grabbing his ankle and twisting it until his foot dangled off his leg. Instead she lied there, realizing that he wouldn't do anything more than touch himself with his foot between her legs until he ejaculated, then creep back to his own room to cry.

When the nuns came to visit in the morning, they only wanted one version of affairs. They smiled and sat with the lady of the house while coffee was served with cookies. Margo appeared with her hair braided neatly and her cotton dress freshly washed. The family's youngest child traipsed in and pulled at her skirt in a display of how attached she was growing to her. The women chatted a bit while Margo stood at attention. Then the boy came in barefoot, dressed in one of Margo's plain work dresses and wrapped his arms around her from behind and said that they were twins. *Regarde, Maman. On est des jumelles!* The nuns dropped their cups and almost choked on their cookies before excusing themselves. They left with Margo in tow, crossing themselves as they went.

The Syrian family that took her in after that was in the importing business and had a mercantile shop in town. After a year as a domestic in their home, she became a stock girl in the shop they ran. She watched Mr. Mamoun manage his staff with an iron hand, wrangle with import officials about shipments, and took lessons on how to be imposing. Occasionally there had been negotiations and strong-arming tactics that no one spoke about, but she knew enough to keep quiet and see without seeing. She was discreet and showed up early to tidy the shop every morning. She kept her hands busy and avoided speaking before being spoken to. Margo proved to be loyal, but she sealed their trust in her the day she saved the owner's only son from choking to death.

Some children had gathered in the store's yard and the boy had come out with a huge plastic bag of marshmallows. They all flocked to him like birds with their hands outstretched. He passed the marshmallows out like a small fat Jesus passing out fish and bread on a riverbank. They ate the sweets with joyful speed cramming them into their gaping mouths and swallowing almost without chewing. The owner's son popped a marshmallow into his own mouth for every few he distributed. His mother and some of her friends sat in the yard talking and giggling at the children's greedy display. Suddenly, the boy stopped passing out the goodies and stood blank-faced holding his chest. His eyes glassed over and his body started hiccupping. The bag fell from his hands and the women started to scream at his reddening face. Margo looked up from counting money at the register. She had been used to the Syrians being loud and having their rows.

Mostly she pretended not to hear them and stayed out of their affairs. But this time there was something desperate in that female screech that sent a sting of alarm crawling over her scalp. She dropped the cash and ran out to the yard.

The boy was convulsing on his side, his swollen cheek pressed into the dirt. The women were shaking him and squeezing his stomach, calling his name. Margo picked up her skirt and in three long steps crossed the yard to where the child lay. With a wave of one hand she scattered the children and commanded the screeching women to step aside. She pulled the boy up by the ankles and shook him upside down like a bag of rice. His face only became redder and his eyes began to bulge. She quickly pressed him belly down over her bent knee and rammed three fingers into his throat. His body gave a violent heave and he regurgitated a flow of sticky white goo onto Margo's hand. She turned him over and wiped his face with the hem of her skirt and sat him upright on the ground. Her face was hard and searching as she rubbed his neck and slapped his back. She squeezed his hands and felt his belly. When the boy's breathing finally steadied, his mother fell to her knees in relief.

Margo gave notice to the Syrians when she realized that she was pregnant a couple of months later. She didn't want to answer questions, though it wasn't likely that there would be any. She had been a fixture at the store for almost ten years and no one wanted to see her go, mystery baby or not. The owner's wife brought her baked goods and set aside perfumes and oils for Margo to choose from at the end of each week trying to change her mind. Margo thanked the wife for the sweet *nahsh* or the sticky *qatayef* with a stoic nod (the boy made quick work of those), but her plans were set. On her last day at the store, she thanked Mr. Mamoun for the education her work in his shop had been. He shook her hand like a man, then without words, quickly touched his forehead to hers and let her walk away.

Back in Jacmel, Margo trekked to larger houses in town selling fabric and sewing services. She worked in her small garden at home but as she filled out, she decided that the door-to-door *Madan Sara* lifestyle wouldn't work for long. She had no one to hand her a glass of lemonade while she fanned herself in the afternoon heat dreaming of baby names. She couldn't afford paralyzing emotion, so she set up her own mercantile shop out of her house. She wore long denim skirts, wrapped her head in scarves, and kept a dagger in her pocket.

At first business was slow. Margo sat behind the rough counter and stared out at the dusty street with a pensive dent in her forehead that seemed to have always been there. Aside from country folk not having much money to spare, they were wary of the shopkeeper and the word of mouth hurt. The talk about Margo kept some people away from the shop for a long time, but she still opened up, swept the floor, and dusted the shelves and rotated the merchandise that she rode to Port-au-Prince for every month. Though women in town finally came in for their children's school supplies, dried mushrooms, or brassieres, they still whispered about how she had gone bald while she was living in Port-au-Prince and that was the reason no one ever saw her hair. Others said that the reason the father of her child was never seen is that she had murdered him as soon as she became pregnant. They said that she served *lwa* and had protection that came from a shack deep in the valley.

On one of those long empty days, she looked over her selection of pipes. The men in the hills who enjoyed a good smoke in the evenings came in and bought them from her. She chose a simple Corn Cob style for herself and rolled it between her fingers, imagining how she would stuff it with tobacco and smoke in celebration after her baby was born. She imagined that she would light her pipe and smoke proudly, filling the store with thick fragrance so heavy that she would open the door to let it spread out over the front steps and into the street and through the ragged brush at the turn of the road and into the valley and over the mountain and over the ocean all the way to *Ginen* where their people all came from. The women there would pause in the sun with their bare feet squeezing the earth and close their eyes to breathe in the rich smell. They would know that the smoke came from Margo's store and that she was announcing the birth of her child. That she was continuing the stories and the smells and the tastes and the sounds that could never be forgotten, even though they were worlds apart.

But Margo didn't smoke her yellow pipe when Parnel was born. She kept it in the pocket of her skirt or hidden in the folds of her head wrap. She didn't start smoking it until ten years had passed and her son was sealed in his child-sized mausoleum.

∾∾

Hélène hadn't always been so nervous. As a girl she'd run through sloping fields with her brother Parnel. They had played soccer in dirt yards and eaten fried fish on the beach with the neighborhood kids in the summer. She had never cared about dress fabrics, and with her short hair, ribbons hadn't mattered to her either. She preferred to share her brother's short pants and cotton shirts when they played. Since they were only eleven months apart and were the same height and build, they played a game where they pretended to be twins. When Hélène would kick a rock with her bare foot, Parnel immediately grabbed his toe, wailing in pain. Hélène would put an entire hot pepper in her mouth and Parnel went into a frenzy looking for water to soothe the fire bursting in his throat. They'd pull this one in the middle of the shop sometimes and the ladies counting out crumpled Gourdes at the cashier would grab their skirts and cry *amwey!* Give him water! Hurry! The two pranksters would run out laughing and didn't stop until they hit the beach. They'd splash into the water up to their waists, then roll around on the shore until their legs were caked with sand. Parnel's skin was caramel while Hélène's was a deeper cocoa. They had never known their father and it was rumored that they didn't share the same one. The talk made no difference to them and it never occurred to them to ask their mother about it.

On the day of Parnel's burial, some women walked with Margo to her family plot. There were some tombs already arranged in a wide pyramid formation. Her forebears rested at the base and she had had her own spot prepared when she had first come back from Port-au-Prince pregnant. The idea was to leave one less worry behind when her time came to join the ancestors, and to familiarize her offspring early with where they would all eventually come home to rest. She had always imagined that she would fill her own before her children's, but that was not to be. Margo stood dry-eyed with nine year-old Hélène at her side, watching a man seal the opening where they had just placed her son. Afterwards, she kissed the girl on the forehead and sent her along with the women who kept patting her shoulder and wiping their own eyes. They wanted to stay with her to offer comfort, but once they saw her squat on a loose cinderblock and stare out into the valley, they understood that she wanted to be left alone. Still, they lingered some yards away, pretending not to watch her. When the sun was just about to retreat below the line of hills in the distance, burning off the last of its fiery rays on the horizon, Margo reached into her pocket and pulled out her pipe. She packed it carefully with tobacco and lit a match.

After Parnel was gone, Hélène no longer wanted to wear his clothes. She started looking for the new dresses that her mother put in her closet every season and asked her to tie ribbons around her short braids. She stopped playing soccer with the neighborhood boys and started following the girls in her class to jump rope and doll games after school instead. She became interested in singing and sewing and spent more and more time listening to the radio and practicing dance steps. In the summer, she worked with her mother at the store cleaning, organizing inventory on the shelves, and digging in the garden. She covered her head with the same cotton wraps that Margo wore, but was quick to take them off as soon as her chores were done. She sat on the cinderblock steps at the bottom of the porch at dusk and carefully flipped through magazines. Her mother carried *Silver Screen* and *Marie Claire* at the store. It was mainly the hotel and bar owners who bought copies to lay around to give a cosmopolitan air to their village storefronts. Some families with money sent a girl in bare feet to buy a copy to keep on a coffee table to impress guests. But mostly they stayed on the shelves. Hélène wiped her fingers on her skirt before lifting the pages to keep from smudging the ink. She memorized the postures of the movie stars on the glossy pages and imagined herself into those poses, those arms and legs folded gracefully under faces etched with security.

As Hélène left girlhood, Margo didn't try to press her into any feminine confines. Many neighborhood women already thought it was strange that she had let her daughter run around in boys' clothes for so long and pitied her having such short hair. Margo preferred to teach her daughter by example. She didn't think twice about slaughtering her own chickens and goats, or building the extension to their house by herself. On the days she waited on the porch for her deliveries to come from the city, she smoked her pipe with a sharpened machete within reach. She leaned it against the wood railing as she got up to pay the driver extra for bringing her items to her door when she couldn't make the trip herself. A nod and a handshake that almost pulled him off balance secured his services for the next month, and he tipped his straw hat before driving off.

Margo sent Hélène to the Catherine Damas girls' school in Port-au-Prince for her secondary studies. It was a trade school for country families who aspired to appear middle class and middle class families who tried to forget their country attachments. The girl was more than pleased to move to a place where she could have her hair pressed regularly and wear little ankle socks with her closed buckle shoes.

On her final summer before graduation she came home accompanied by a tall young man in a starched soldier's uniform. Margo sat on the store porch watching them come up the road. Hélène wore a yellow dress with white gloves and a straw sun hat. As they approached, the two did not touch until he held out his arm to help her up the few cement steps leading to the railing. Margo knew what the conversation would be before either of them said a word. Edgar Séjour's eyes were small and sharp, and his full lips were squeezed into a polite purse that she did not trust. His large hands were hard, but that was to be expected for a military man. Still, Margo felt something unsettling in the touch of his palm against hers when they shook hands. It was a scratch like sandpaper or dry brush.

Hélène had already accepted his proposal and they wanted her blessing before they started planning. Margo offered Edgar a cup of coffee and took Hélène inside to talk. Where were his people from? Had she visited them and learned about how he grew up? The North. A vague reference to region, not an actual town, no particular homestead. He told her that he had been strong enough to make a good life for himself and he would apply that strength to making a good life for the two of them, if she gave him a chance. He told her she was the kind of girl he had always dreamed of meeting. Someone to smooth his hard edges with her natural elegance. Someone who understood what it meant to need someone else, and who would need him more than anyone else. Margo furrowed her brow and tried to warn her daughter about men who didn't honor the earth they came from and thought they could stand against a hurricane and force it to blow over and around them without ever making them lean. But there was no point.

After the solemn military wedding ceremony where the bride and groom walked back down the aisle under an arch of raised swords in the *Église Sacré Coeur de Turgeau*, after the brief honeymoon getaway at the Eriksson and their settling in a cottage in Petionville, after their three girls were born and their move to a grand house in Pacot, Hélène couldn't possibly tell her mother how things really were. She coiled into herself under layers of linen dresses, silk stockings, sun hats, soft cotton sheets, perfumes and cosmetics imported from France until she was buried too comfortably to ever come out. Early on, before Margo retreated into parental isolationism, she had responded to one of

Hélène's bland letters with only one line as a final admonishment.

"Dry wood catches fire, my daughter. And you've made your home far from the water."

∂∞∂

By day thirty in Margo's strange countdown, her routine of silence with Edgar had become so efficient that they never had to exchange more than ten words a day when he was home. *Bonjour, Colonel. Bonsoir, Impératrice.* Neither one seemed the least bothered by the distance, but it was driving Hélène crazy--except that since her mother had arrived, the bruises on her jaw and on her shoulders had faded and no new ones had come to take their place.

It was almost the end of the school year and the girls were getting antsy. There were constant requests for special desserts to take to school or for afternoon visits with classmates. The Séjour girls were not allowed to visit friends at their homes and Edgar barely tolerated when their friends came to them. He sat silently behind his book in the parlor and the girls knew to keep from irritating him with questions. Hélène would walk the halls, stopping in the doorways and stand quietly, memorizing the walls, the chairs, the shelves, even the curtains and how they rose in the breeze. She would disappear into the bathroom and spend an hour washing her face and applying her make up over and over again. A fresh face made her a fresh person who could handle the silent pressure that was closing in with each passing day. But after more than ten years of this routine, she only emerged looking more frazzled, with the skin on her face and neck looking like it belonged to two different people.

The trip to New York was Hélène's idea. It came to her in the kitchen one morning while she gathered ingredients for a pie. Mimose was going to the bakery early to pick up some rolls and patties the girls had been clamoring for, but Hélène insisted on making something herself. She was tired of inspecting already made beds and opening closet doors to find shoes arranged in neat rows and dresses hanging by color. Especially with her mother around, it was difficult to stay idle. Maintaining an appearance of being busy was exhausting and made her ache for actual work.

She sprinkled flour and salt on the granite counter and bent her head over the dough she kneaded with an intensity that turned her small hands into weapons. She dug her knuckles in gently at first, and then as she pressed and rolled, her elbows came up and down propelling her fists like hammers. The dough became a face that she bludgeoned and broke apart by blows. The crease in her brow deepened and perspiration flattened her curls. Margo's sandaled feet made no sound as she stepped into the kitchen and even as she pulled out a chair to sit. Hélène never broke focus on punishing the dough.

"What are you going to do with these girls for the summer?"

Hélène jumped and turned to find her mother sitting at the kitchen table, staring out at the yard through the open back door. Margo had a habit of asking a question without seeming to expect an answer. Maybe she already knew the answer and wanted to see if the one she received would be in line with the one she had already accepted. Hélène turned back to wrap her dough and put it away to settle in the freezer.

"I haven't spoken to Edgar about that yet. He hasn't even been home that long and it looks like he'll have to go back to the capital soon."

"Yes, Papa Doc has all his men on call these days."

Hélène froze. Her lips parted for a few trembling seconds, but closed again. The accusation in Margo's tone was too poorly veiled. Hélène wanted to turn around and remind her mother that she was a guest in her home and that hostility towards her husband or any questioning of his position would not be tolerated. There was no reason they couldn't exist together under the same roof for the duration of her visit without fighting. But that was just it. There had been no fights. Her mother and husband barely even spoke, and the girls embraced her even though they were practically strangers. They had only seen her once or twice when they were babies, and Mathilda had never met her at all. With every letter Hélène wrote, the little one was always so eager to sign in her own hand so her grandmother would recognize some piece of her.

"Mama, please, I don't want *granmanman* to forget me!"

"Mathilda, your grandmother could never forget you. You don't forget people when they belong to you."

The words came out of Hélène's mouth with such easy dismissal that she paused after they were said. She looked into her daughter's face and thought about how to claim those eyes, that mouth, that jutting chin. She bit her lip when she came up with nothing. Hélène wanted to scream to her mother that she should show more respect, that

Edgar was a good husband and a strong father for the girls and that she would have never had a life like this if she hadn't married him. They were all lucky to have him as their protector. Instead, she reached for a bowl of ripe peaches and started cutting them into quarters, digging out the ridged pits, and peeling the thin skin from their flesh. Margo dragged on her pipe, still looking out at the Mimosa bowing in the yard.

"I heard they're finishing renovations on the American school," Margo said. "Those people they have teaching sound like cracked wheels rolling over rocks when they try to speak French."

"Marie Lourdes already started her English class at Saint Francois D'Assise."

"And the other two?"

"The same person will teach them next year."

"That eighty-five-year-old French nun?"

"*Oui.*"

"If you dropped that woman in New York she would teach everyone she met to speak French instead of learning another word of English."

Hélène shrugged and they went on like this. She pouring sugar and vanilla on the glistening peach wedges, and Margo exhaling pipe smoke at the back door and making her comments to the breeze.

Hélène could hear the girls giggling and chanting as they came in from seeing a movie with Mimose. After a year of practicing English, Marie Lourdes taught her sisters that "The End" was pronounced *tay uhnd*. Hélène had an idea.

"I wonder what Edgar would say about a trip to Miami." Margo sucked her teeth. "You might as well stay here."

"Well, then... New York."

"Hmm." Margo chewed her pipe as she watched the sun start to climb down his ladder in the sky. Hélène picked up a rolling pin and started spreading out the dough.

❧

The girls couldn't contain their excitement the morning of the big trip. They wouldn't hold still long enough for Mimose to comb their hair into their usual five braids tipped with butterfly barrettes.

"Mimose, can you do our hair in *chou*? Please, please?" asked Marie Lourdes.

"Oh, yes, yes, yes! Please!" Madeleine chimed in.

"That's for special occasions, girls. Fancy."

"But we're going in an airplane, Mimose! We're

going to be in the sky! I want God to see me looking special when I fly." Mathilda said.

"God sees you all the time, *ti-piti*. He sees all things, even way down here."

"Oh, Mimose *tanpri!!!*

She gave in and brushed their masses of black hair into smooth buns secured with a clear bubble tie and a satin ribbon. She carefully brushed the fine baby hair to frame their faces and set it with her saliva-wet thumb. She helped the girls into their church dresses, complete with ankle socks with lace trim, and white patent-leather shoes.

"Here, hold your gloves until you get in the car. You don't want your fingers to be black before you even get to the airport."

They grabbed their dainty white gloves and scampered out, barely catching their excited breaths. Madeleine lingered for a moment longer.

"Mimose, do you think Papa will be back before we leave?"

"I don't think so, *cocotte*."

Outside the sun was crashing against the house. Margo bent down to rip up a few weeds popping through the cobblestones and tossed them into the road. She rubbed her face vigorously and stood at the gate watching Hélène supervise the loading of the car. She took her pipe from her pocket and started stuffing it with tobacco. The girls came running out of the house and hovered around the car skipping and singing. Mathilda wrapped her arms around her grandmother's waist and stared up at her like a puppy.

"*Grandmanman*, what should I bring you back from New York?"

Margo loved the innocence in her granddaughter's face and feared it at the same time.

"Bring me a pipe."

"You have a pipe already!"

Margo bent down and met Mathilda nose to nose and whispered, "I think I'll need another one soon." Mathilda nuzzled into her grandmother's neck.

"I'll get you a red one!"

"Yes, bring a red pipe home to me. Now go!"

She scampered off and Margo stayed by the gate watching her climb into the car after her sisters. They giggled and shoved each other in the backseat while Hélène packed one last bag into the trunk. She went slowly, counting her movements and adding them up in her head. She never came up with the right number so she started over, opening the trunk again or checking her purse for passports and birth certificates for the hundredth time.

"*Madan* Séjour, we have to get going. Don't want

you to be late for your plane."

Hélène broke out of her trance and looked up at Babo, the driver. She forced a smile and nodded. Edgar was at a post in the northeast and would not be home until that night. He had reminded the girls to practice and come back with at least one pleasing phrase memorized in perfect English. He did not have any special requests for his wife, though Hélène knew to look for the designer silk ties and suspenders he liked. Babo slipped off his shoes and smacked them together before putting them back on and getting behind the wheel. Hélène couldn't procrastinate any longer. She smoothed her hair and adjusted the strap of her shoulder bag. She walked over to her mother who was waiting like the guardian of a doomed palace.

"Mr. Mamoun's son is meeting us at the airport, right?" Hélène asked.

Margo drew from her pipe and nodded.

"How will I know him?"

"He's a fat Syrian. And he will know you."

Hélène wanted to say something more, but she couldn't find her words. Something rolling in the pit of her stomach kept her from breathing too deeply or looking up.

"OK then, *Manman*. We're going."

Margo quickly circled one arm around her daughter's shoulders and pulled her close in a way that she had not done since she was a little girl, still wearing her brother's shirts and short pants. She cradled Hélène's face to her own, and rocked for a long moment. Then she whispered in her ear.

"One."

Hélène pulled back and stared into her mother's eyes. She had known from the day Margo arrived at her door that there was something, a reason for this counting of days, but had never asked for an explanation. She still didn't want to know, but she felt it there between them in that moment like an invisible hand pulling them apart before it was time. The lines around the eyes crinkled. A sigh settled deep in the throat. She backed slowly away to the car and got in on the passenger side. The girls babbled about learning to speak English and eating hot dogs and candy. From the front seat Hélène turned to see her mother and her house getting smaller and smaller, until they were gone.

꙾

That night the air in the Pacot hills was unusually warm and dry. The drooping palm and banana leaves hissed as they rubbed together in the breeze and the earth along the road was dusty and pale.

After the sun had set, the neighborhood got very quiet. Even the dogs had tucked themselves out of sight. Servants were in their quarters, and all husbands were accounted for in parlors with newspapers and music, or on verandas smoking. Even the cicadas turned down the volume of their singing.

When Babo came back from the airport in the afternoon, he had found parcels lined up at the gate. There were bags of rice, dry beans, salt, sugar, cured meat, spices, and seeds for the yard man's family on the side of the mountain. There were shoes, socks, and a heavy tarp rolled and tied with rope for Babo. There were healing oils, dry leaves in small paper bags, yards of white cotton, and a shiny pair of scissors for the cook. Mimose's payment came in an envelope filled with one thousand dollars in American cash and a letter.

When Edgar came home that night, a fresh bottle of Barbancourt and a clean glass waited for him on the kitchen table. He unscrewed the cap and raised the bottle to his lips. The heat trickling down his throat and into his belly erased the question about the bottle being there at all as he looked around the kitchen. The porcelain mixing bowls were stacked and arranged on the open shelves. Every counter was cleared and the kitchen looked as if it had not been used in months. Even the big aluminum pots that usually stayed outside were piled on top of the refrigerator and its hum seemed to have faded to a whisper. He checked inside and found no plate saved for him, but it didn't matter.

He walked through the mute house with his five-star bottle. As he went, he removed piece after piece of his uniform and left it where it lay. He took off his boots near the kitchen table and dropped his hat on the floor next to them. He left his tie on the counter, tossed his shirt in the hallway, and flung his belt on the parlor floor. The stiff stride he usually came in with had turned into an amble and by the time he reached the bedroom he shared with his wife, he was naked as the day he was born. He reclined on his bed, took another swallow from the bottle and began to sing. *"La rose et le muget, fleur soleil, chevalier de nuit..."* He sang out, but his voice didn't travel very far. The still air refused to carry it beyond a few feet away from him. The silence of the night sucked in every sound except the steady cracking of twigs in the brush behind the house and the rustle of heavy denim that he couldn't hear even if he had been listening. He sang out and waited for her. He wanted her to come in and find him intoxicated, lying in wait. He had left the gate unlocked and the front door slightly open so she could get in on her own. This would be her first time in his grand house, rather than her small apartment in the city. He took another swallow and lolled on the cotton sheets. He didn't notice the lemony herb smell that sat quiet in the corners, waiting for the right time to mingle with the night air that would soon crawl deep into his lungs. Hélène was always trying new combinations of herbs and oils to freshen the house and that was one thing Edgar rather liked. No matter how far she came from the dirt trails around her mother's home in Jacmel's valley, some things Hélène could never leave behind. Like how to use the plants that took over her garden and the land beyond the house. Her fingers remembered how to handle cinnamon, cloves, lemon and orange peel, and fresh mint to make mixtures for the different spaces in their home. The dabs of lilac or lavender behind her ears moved with her from room to room, and her sachets anchored her presence whether she was there or not. This night those smells were gone. All were absent except for one. It was quiet Sage, whispering in the parlor, in the kitchen, in each bedroom, even in the bathrooms and on the patio, waiting for the moment to swell up to the ceiling and against the windows, pushing outward with nowhere left to go before curling back in. Edgar might have raised an eyebrow, if he had noticed, if it had mattered.

But his wife was not on his mind that night. The trail of discarded clothing would lead another woman to his bed that night. He kept sipping from the bottle at his bedside until the words of his song dripped from his tongue like syrup. He fought hard against the rum-laced drowsiness so he would be alert for her, but after a while his eyes couldn't help but close. He tossed with slurred impatience, but the woman he was waiting for never arrived.

The woman who did come brought flames on her fingertips that swallowed the house whole.

Haitian legends can be full of holes, but they do die hard. Hélène and her girls were eventually traced to New York, alive and well, and starting new lives. The army had opened an investigation about the fire, but closed it quickly since there were no complainants and no witnesses to corroborate or dispute any evidence of arson. They tried to locate the servants who had worked at the Séjour house for questioning, but none were found. Hurricane Flora came a few months later and the devastation that spread over every house for miles around made everything else irrelevant. It seemed anyone who knew the family had perished, melted into the valley, or crawled back up the mountains to pick up some thin threads of life. Madame Séjour had no living siblings and her mother, Margonne Impératrice, was presumed dead since she had been staying with the family and did not travel with them when they left. Col. Séjour's distant relatives in the north didn't even know that he had been married and had not seen him for more than thirty years. People throughout Pacot, Petionville, Turgeau, and Laboule whispered that Hélène's mother, the hard old woman who came to stay with them that summer and who was thought to have also perished (either in the fire or during the hurricane, depending on who you spoke to), could be seen haunting the skeleton of that grand house behind locked gates some nights. Some say they've seen her dressed in white, roaming the empty hill and the land behind it in the dark, stepping over the rubble and brush. Others say they've seen her sitting in a low wooden chair among the ruins, smoking a red pipe.

Sometimes she's spotted walking in the ravine at the edge of town early in the morning, her long denim skirt dragging, her sandaled feet stepping at a deliberate pace. She leaves a trail of sweet tobacco in her wake.

3 Carly

I was still in Jordache jeans and pink
KangaROOS sneakers when I lost my
mother. In those days I pulled mesh tank tops over
a Sesame Street T-shirt and stacked more than
twenty rubber bracelets in all colors on my wrists,
trying to imitate Madonna. I wrapped an oversized
Hello Kitty belt around my non-existent hips and
danced to music videos when I was supposed to be
doing homework.

   She started disappearing slowly, when I wasn't
looking, like water going down a slow drain. But
even if I had been staring straight on, everything

was covered in a haze that my eyes were not equipped to see through.

When company came over on the weekends after church, family friends gossiping about other family friends, Grandma Hélène would set paper napkins on her old lace tablecloth and give an apologetic smile about the loud music or the occasional *nam myoho renge kyo* chanting coming from the other side of the bedroom door. The guests ate their patties and sipped their coffee making mental notes about what they would talk about on their next social stop. Things hadn't changed much from Port-au-Prince, only the parlor was now a corner of a cramped one-bedroom apartment and the matrons were even fatter. They wore cheap polyester dresses and rubber soled shoes and synthetic wigs on their heads instead of hats. Grandma Hélène didn't go to church anymore. Instead she woke up early on Sundays and put on her Soft Cocoa foundation to the tune of whatever was playing on the Haitian channel, so long as it was in French. She dressed in wool and tweed in the winter and linen in summer, and lit candles while she waited for her regular visitors to come after service.

During the day, while I was at school, Grandma turned the television way up so that the voice of

Bob Barker or Richard Dawson distracted from the weirdness of my mother's pacing with some game show excitement. She called out to the screen and cheered with the contestants when they shared correct answers, like she was the one helping them win. She knotted her lips and crossed her arms tight across her chest when they got answers wrong and eventually lost. In the evenings, she smiled with satisfaction as Vanna White turned each letter on the board across the screen to spell out words she was still learning how to pronounce. Sometimes my mother went along with the game and repeated the winning phrase, "A Stitch in Time Saves Nine" "Little Red Riding Hood" "High Fructose Corn Syrup." Grandma Hélène got used to pretending to ignore my mother's wild moods because words like Bipolar Disorder or Paranoid Schizophrenia simply didn't exist in our lexicon. All I know is that something crept in like a hooded thief in the night and stole my mother away, and for so many years, no one rang the alarm.

I think I had her for a while, maybe when I was really little, in moments so far gone that I'm not allowed to access them. When I finally had the courage to go through the cardboard boxes of stuff she had piled in her room, I found some pictures of me squirming in her arms, laughing and pointing at the camera. I don't doubt that she was awake and present in those days. She had her arms wrapped around me with a look of quiet joy, like there was no better place for either of us to be. The pictures are the proof, aren't they? They prove that she was real. They capture her as she was, dazzling and fresh, at that time anyway. Today she sits at the bottom of a well, her face quivering somewhere in the depths. And no matter how many times I dive in, she's always too far to reach.

It was the strength of my will that kept her alive in the darkest days, but it takes more than a child's will and I couldn't be there all the time. I lost count of how many times I complained of stomachaches and pressed hot washcloths against my face to fake fevers. After a while she got wise to my game, and sent me off to school no matter how much I whined. I worried when I was away from her. I enjoyed spending weekends at my dad's house, but while I was there sometimes I caught myself chewing the soft inside of my cheeks until it was raw and burned when I drank Dr. Peppers. I'd imagine all sorts of scenarios: her standing alone in the silence of our living room, driving a knife into her own belly, putting the barrel of a gun into her mouth, or running across an expressway with her eyes closed. But that's not how she died.

❧❦

The first time I called my mother Carly she stopped dancing and looked at me like we were meeting for the very first time. She had been practicing Solid Gold dance moves in between folding piles of laundry.

"What?"

"I said when are we having dinner? I'm hungry. Can we order from the..."

"Who told you to call me that?"

It was from a picture I found in her jewelry box under a pile of bracelets and beads she hadn't worn in forever. It was old and they were cradling each other's afros, gazing, lost in love. The dedication on the back was in her curly scribble: *To Dorly, from your loving Carly.*

She wasn't upset, just perplexed and intensely interested in what I would say next. Her reaction was so strong that I knew I had to come up with something memorable. So, I paused and took a breath before answering.

"Oh, it's just something I came across somewhere. I know, I know, even before me, you were magical. You were *Carly*."

I said it with a flourish and dimmed eyes, flouncing to her side. I took a sweater out of her hands and finished folding it. Her face melted into a smile that erased whatever question it might have worn and she pulled me into her arms with urgency.

"I love it. Call me that all the time."

Carly was a dream. Her skin looked like chocolate milk in a clear glass and she had the most beautiful white teeth I had ever seen. Better than a Crest commercial. They were big, but not too big. They looked like a proud row of white squares, standing against each other with discipline, ready for anything. You couldn't help staring at them when she talked or sang words like *"Oui Monsieur la petite Marie, est tellement tellement jolie."* Her full lips, the ones I didn't get, pulled up into a smile no matter what the lyrics were. She never took formal dance classes, but she had the legs; those I did get. Sometimes she would sing and prance from room to room of our apartment as if she were stepping on lily pads in a perfect *pas de chat*. She'd suddenly kick up high past her shoulder, do a twirl, and raise her finger as if she were about to make a grand point, stare off into the distance... then break into laughter, totally teasing. I got caught up in the magic every time. I followed her around waiting for a finale that was sure to be accompanied by violins or trumpets, and was always blown away when it came.

My father had been blown away too when they met. They both had day jobs and took night classes at Brooklyn College. Carly was rehearsing her monologue for a production of *Othello* in an empty room in the Student Union building and he was coming from a particularly skull cracking economics exam, looking for a place have his coffee before heading to another class. He shuffled down the hall past an open door and saw her posturing, standing her ground to her father for the love of a Moor. Her respectful plea for understanding was so heartfelt that the words stopped being lines in a play and became a message of devotion from the fiery-eyed beauty, directly to him. He forgot the watery coffee in his one hand, the cheap briefcase in the other and almost expected to hear a response from the Venetian senator to his staunch daughter. The imitation leather handle slid in his sweaty palm and he turned into a page at her side, ready to follow her to anywhere their heavy island accents could declaim English poetry without losing an ounce of its grandeur.

He loved her before she was even aware of him. His heart knelt to the military square of her shoulders, the throaty timbre of her voice, the wide spread of fingers that made her every gesture reach into the corners of the room and fill it with vibration. When she finally turned around, her dark eyes hit him with a gaze that was electric and melancholy at the same time. That was her power. That's how Carly captured everyone. She pulled you in to the magic thing in her that was already sleeping in you, and you became hers. But in the end they were just too different. The opposites attract thing didn't work the way it did in romantic comedies. They spoke the same language, they had roots in the same small town in Jacmel, and they both knew the value of grapefruit peel tea sprinkled with salt, but they were worlds apart. She was a theater major and was passionate about an acting career. He studied economics and was far more practical.

"Mathilda, I don't want to have this conversation. Immigrants cannot afford to chase crazy dreams. They barely give jobs as it is. You want to make things more difficult for us?"

"Samuel, that's not fair! You can't expect me to do something I hate my whole life just because I'm an immigrant! At what point do we stop being immigrants?"

"Never! And what's wrong with being a nurse? A nurse can always find a job, no matter how bad times are. People are always sick."

"Samuel, you're not listening to me!"

Things got really bad when he gave her an ultimatum about going back to school and taking a job as a secretary in the office of the Haitian doctor around the corner on Cortelyou Road. He gave his edict as if he had been handing them out all his life, confident that it would be followed. There was yelling and nostrils flaring and feet stamping, but the harder he pushed the more Carly refused to bend to his will.

"Let me tell you something, Samuel Séraphin, my father died when I was ten, okay? I wasn't shopping for another one on my wedding day!"

As soon as the words left her mouth, he slapped it. His hand had flown up and whipped against her face to both of their surprise. They stood staring at each other without breathing and the next words to fill the silent space between their lean bodies were,

"I'm pregnant."

She did end up taking the job at the doctor's office. The work was mindless shuffling of papers day in and day out. She smiled and set calendars, processed bills, and ordered supplies. She stayed until almost a week before her due date and soon after I learned to walk, she filed for divorce and we went to live with Grandma Hélène on the Upper West Side.

❧✦

"Baby, come here! Quick!"

I had just come in from school and Carly was sitting cross-legged on the living room floor in harem pants and a cowboy shirt.

"Come, come, come! Come, baby, look at this!"

I dumped my book bag and knelt beside her as she sifted through papers strewn on the floor in front of her.

"What is it, Carly? Are we in trouble?"

"In trouble? You're crazy! Look, look..."

She picked up a few typed pages folded in threes and pointed to various paragraphs and signatures. She tossed them in the air and jumped up laughing, skipping around like an elf. I barely saw any of the words she pointed out but skipped along with her, confused and excited at once. Grandma Hélène came down the hall with a cup of tea in her hands. She took short steps to keep it from spilling onto the saucer.

"What's happen in here?"

"I got a show, *Manman,* a big show! This is it! This is finally it!" Carly grabbed my hands and twirled me until I got dizzy. Grandma dabbed her lipstick with a tissue before taking a sip of her tea, and shook her head at us.

"*Manman,* you can't tell me this is not exciting! You think I should keep tutoring brats forever? Serving coffee somewhere? Typing in an office?"

Carly had landed one of the lead roles in a Broadway production full of black women singing in glittering gowns and changing wigs. It was perfect because out of all the roles I had watched her rehearse and perform on stage, this one was the most like her. I remember thinking I could watch the whole thing with no sound and still see Carly through the makeup and costumes. Her expressions, her voice, and gestures were all the same. Grandma sighed and smoothed her skirt behind her before sitting on the couch, ankles crossed.

"Working in an office is more secure, and safer than being out so late."

"Safer? What does that even mean? Come on, you know this is an exciting opportunity…"

"If your father was alive, he would agree with me."

"Dammit, *Manman!* If Papa was alive we wouldn't be here at all! We'd be locked up in our fancy house holding our breath, waiting for someone to burn us alive."

Grandma Hélène's lips pursed to a thin line and her hand shook, spilling a bit of tea in her lap. Carly hurried over and scrambled to her knees. It was only a few drops, but I watched her keep wiping and straightening her mother's skirt over and over. Grandma put her cup down and lifted Carly's chin.

"If your papa was here, he would not know you."

Carly looked up at her mother with eyes trembling with frustration, but kept her voice soft.

"*Manman,* we never knew him. And he never knew us. But it doesn't matter because I know me. I know how to fly."

৵৽৽

On opening night I walked around the lobby of the Lighthouse Theatre with a ticket in my hand. I wore a black velvet dress trimmed in pink satin that Carly had laid out for me with matching ribbons in my hair, but I drew the line at the lacy ankle socks. I suppose that was the finishing touch to Sunday best dressing when she was a kid. I saw other girls at school sporting them on picture day, but I was not interested.

"*Manmi*, can I just wear stockings?" It was always *Manmi* when I really wanted something. "The little socks are so... babyish!"

"But, baby... I mean, Ollie, they look so pretty with the dress! C'mon..."

"*Manmi*, please, I promise I'll wear them for my communion. But not tonight!"

"Olive..."

"Stockings will be more magical."

I gave her wide eyes and a smile that she would have given, a smile I had seen her flash on stage a million times during rehearsals to cajole a co-star, or to soften the director, and it worked.

"Well, we can certainly use all the magic we can get tonight. You can wear your pink tights." I gave in to the compromise.

In the lobby I slipped between adults dressed in suits and satin dresses with shoulder pads. I knew where my seat was in the front row, but I wanted to be seen wearing my pretty outfit, the only child among adults, and be asked what I was doing there. I strolled proudly, trying to make eye contact with anyone who passed me as the crowd milled. When someone, predictably, asked if I was lost, I responded, that my mother knew where I was.

When they asked where my mother was, I pointed her out on the life-sized poster near the entrance, "The one on the left. She's backstage getting ready", their mouths hung open and I walked off, smug as a bug.

I crept through the double doors that led to the backstage area and went to the dressing room Carly shared with the other two leads. She was sitting in front of her mirror applying strokes of mascara to her false lashes. She turned just as I stepped into the room like she expected me to come in at that very moment, and stopped me in my tracks with one look. She was a vision draped in blue silk and feathers. Her beehive wig was piled high and secured with gold pins. The make up was like a mask, but her dark eyes still glinted at anyone who fell in their line of fire. I was transfixed.

"Darling, I was waiting. You know I can't go on without you."

She gave an offended tone and held my stare. Of course I knew she was acting. I knew that when she was on stage she was playing a role that was rehearsed to death. But there was no way that it was all pretend. When she sashayed, with her shoulders back, led with her chin, and said her lines in those fierce tones with those wide gestures, she magnified herself. In those small dressing rooms polishing her makeup, when she gripped me with her gaze, I couldn't speak. I barely breathed at all and the only thing I could think of doing was to bow. I gave her a slow curtsy with my heart pounding up my throat. She broke into a smile and beckoned me over for a kiss. In that moment I lived ten times the excitement I was sure the audience would feel when she served it to them from the middle of a burning spotlight on stage.

An assistant ushered me to my seat and I let myself melt into the red velvet chair. The hum of voices hushed as the room went dark and the first stage lights came on. The invisible orchestra purred its first notes and the audience held its breath. I attended many performances in those days, even on weeknights. Though I knew the temperature of the room and the timing of the lights and the coming of every note, those first moments sitting in the dark waiting for the spotlight to shine on her walking across the stage were always new. The magic of those few minutes never got old and they made me completely happy.

འ⊸

I remember spending endless hours in the mirror staring at my face. When I was being funny, I made up commercials and practiced them over and over. I once wasted more than half a bottle of Keri doing a lotion commercial in the mirror. I gave my best Grandma Hélène smile as I pumped some into my hand and ceremoniously massaged it onto my arm, then held the bottle up to my face announcing, "Keri, the only choice for smooth skin." When I was being dramatic, I conjured a trickle of soulful tears inspired by the many performances I had seen Carly give. I tried to walk like her, stepping through clouds careful not to disturb their shapes. I draped one of her long skirts over my shoulders like a cape and posed. Even in our most mundane moments at home like putting away groceries or scrubbing the tub, she sprinkled a kind of glitter over everything and made it special.

She read to me at night from *Tintin* comic books and made all the voices. She switched effortlessly from the gruff, whiskey-swilling Captain Haddock, to the absentminded Professor Tournesol, to the wisecracking dog Milou, and we were transported right into the adventures on those colorful pages. These were our moments that no one else could intrude on. We had code names for each other like "biggie" and "smallie", and she let me roller skate in the apartment since the uncarpeted floors were soundproof.

My mother liked to pick me up from school when she could, but she was late so often that I started going to the after-school program. When she was late even for that, it was a problem. On one of those times, I was the only child left and one of the two monitors on staff was none too pleased to be waiting in the front hall with me. She didn't help me with my homework and didn't ask me if I was hungry. She was wedged into a plastic folding chair reading a glossy tabloid about celebrity divorces and designer weight loss drinks, turning the pages with forceful flips. I had started counting those flips and on what seemed like the hundredth one, Carly came rushing in, her shawl tossed over her shoulder. She swept over to kiss me and I got busy gathering my books and pencils. She apologized to the monitor for being late and hurried me along, but the wedged woman was not letting her off that easily. She took in my mother's leather boots, her long wool skirt, cashmere turtleneck, wooden bracelets, the dramatic shawl, her bare face, and short afro. She rolled her eyes and started in.

"I don't know if you realize how long we been sittin' here waiting for you to show up. I mean everybody got things to do and everything, but this ain't no private babysitting service…"

We waited as the woman continued to complain, jabbing her palm with her index finger, her neck craned forward. My mother stood perfectly still with her back straight and her eyes narrowed, gripping my wrist. I shifted in my shoes.

"I'm not tryna say you irresponsible or nothing, but..."

As soon as the woman paused to take a breath, Carly took over.

"I'm so happy to see the quality of person who is watching over my child after school while I struggle to make a living. Have you stopped to think about how it makes this little girl feel when the people looking after her treat her as if she is a burden? Is that how you earned such a high opinion of yourself and your value? She is sitting on those cold marble steps while you are on a proper chair! Yes, I am late. But you are getting paid to do what you doing, are you not? Oh, but you are not paid to care, that is clear!"

Without giving the slack-jawed monitor a chance to respond, Carly reached into her purse, pulled out a twenty-dollar bill and threw it at her.

"Here's a tip for your trouble. Olive, *viens!*"

She yanked me along, leaving the woman still pressed into her chair. As we reached the heavy double doors and were about to push through them, Carly whirled around for a final cutting statement,

"Espèce de chienne! Vous n'avez jamais eu d'enfants!"

And with that we were off. We stomped into the street and down the block towards the closest subway station like marching band warriors. I could hear a full orchestra marking the pounding of our steps with drums, trumpets, and cymbals. At the bottom of the steps, Carly slipped her token in the slot and I knew to scramble under the big yellow turnstile. A bum lounging on the floor near a trashcan looked up as we passed, vibrating from the booming soundtrack in our steps and indignant fire in our eyes. The platform below was long and empty, and the northbound train was nowhere in sight. There was a man lurking at the other end and I couldn't tell if he was minding his own business or looking for a victim.

Carly was still full of music and couldn't slow down. Her hand was wrapped tight around my wrist and she marched us straight towards him, humming absently, not seeing him at all. The closer we got, the more terrified I became. I could make out that his eyes were beady and his longish hair was slicked down the side of his face. The buttons on his jacket were all missing and his hands were hidden deep in his pockets. I tried to slow us down, but Carly kept stepping forward. I looked around to see if there was anyone who would help if the lurking man pulled out a knife or grabbed at my mother, but there was no one. We were alone. My heart was pounding in my throat and I couldn't hear anything but the muffled rumble of a train coming making me dizzy and stiff.

I thought about the pencils in the front pocket of my backpack and tried to figure out how to quickly reach the zipper behind me. I thought about grabbing two or three of those pencils, holding them together like a makeshift dagger, and bringing the sharpened lead points down hard into his thigh or his stomach and dragging my mother to safety. The rumbling in my ears got louder still and I could swear the dirty man with brown teeth was sneering at me. When there was no more than ten feet of space between us, I snatched my arm away from Carly, dropped to the floor, and furiously ripped open my schoolbag. A mighty rush of wind the temperature of breath swept a few loose pages from my homework folder and scattered them across the platform, and before I knew it Carly had caught me by the elbow and pulled me and my disheveled book bag through the open doors of the train.

She chose a two-seater for us, totally oblivious to my panic. The creepy man with brown teeth leaned against the pole on the platform and watched us through the closing doors. Carly had no idea of how close we'd come to being mugged or murdered. We sat on that subway car for another hour before reaching home. She kept her legs crossed and her arm around me, in character, the whole way.

❧

We moved into a beautiful apartment on the Upper East Side where there was a balcony and I had my own room. We kept potted plants on a table in the living room. Ferns, rubber plants, a spider plant, a weeping fig. I took my Barbies on adventures through my little jungle and used my roller skates as cars. Carly would teach me dance routines on weekends and we'd snack on Nabisco saltines with caviar and orange juice.

We had people over for artsy get-togethers where everyone would sit on cushions scattered on the floor. Carly served trays of fancy store-bought hors d'oeuvres with wine and beer. Her friends came with their instruments and broke into impromptu jams of show tunes and old ballads. They would discuss Haitian writers like Morrisseau

Leroy and argue about folk singers exiled from the island for criticizing the government.

They would drink and smoke and laugh and never care that I was sitting among them. One time someone asked me if I could sing like my mother. I stood up and proclaimed all brassy that my mother got her talent from me. They cheered as I performed French ditties and top forty hits that my mother and I sang while we washed dishes together. Everyone applauded, and I bowed gracefully like an honorary member of the troupe. I never wanted to leave those parties to go to bed. I drank soda and nibbled on chocolates and nuts, but I couldn't help but nod off in a corner after a while. Someone would notice me curled up on some cushions and my mother would gather me in her arms to take me to bed. The music would flow on but at a slightly lower volume. In those days I felt like a little muse living in a world of art and music and magic.

The golden days did have an underside of green. Carly had so many new friends and they had their own parties at places an eight-year-old couldn't go. She was spending money as fast as she made it and I spent more and more time with babysitters. They were usually young women who had just arrived in the country and hadn't yet secured the papers or language skills to get a documented job. Often it was someone's cousin or niece for whom my mom was doing a favor by paying them a couple hundred dollars a week to watch me every day after school.

The girls were nice enough, they never did anything that was really wrong, but I always found fault with them. One girl was too quiet and did nothing but follow me around. When I went to the bathroom, she waited outside the closed door until I came out. When I did my homework at the desk in my room, she sat on my bed picking the polish off her nails. I complained to my mother that the girl gave me the creeps and she simply didn't ask her back. Another one talked too much and actually kept me from finishing my homework. She wanted to practice her English and asked me to translate the dialogue on TV shows. She rattled on and on about the caramel sweets she used to make for the kids she took care of in Haiti, and whined that all the kids in New York wanted were Twinkies and potato chips.

The last one didn't speak any English and kept shuttling us back and forth between the apartment and a payphone around the corner. She bought long-distance cards so she could make various calls every evening. I kept wiggling my hand out of her grip because I wanted to stand alongside her like a grownup. I was eight and certainly not liable to wander off and get lost. But she wasn't taking any chances and wrapped her fingers around my wrist and clamped them tight like a handcuff. I rolled my eyes and huffed as she squeezed me as close to her as possible in the half booth and whimpered into the phone. I never really paid attention to what she was saying because I was too annoyed that I was missing Laverne and Shirley. I thought of complaining to my mother, but in the end I felt sorry for the weepy girl. There was something so desperate in the way she hunched her shoulders to press the phone to her ear while she dialed the numbers on the card. There seemed to be an endless reserve of tears ready to roll down her face as soon as the person on the other end picked up. Her voice never went above a plaintive mumble, questioning, begging. I offered her the use of our phone in the kitchen, but she always refused. Eventually, she went away on her own. I don't remember her name, but I never forgot her mournful eyes. I never told about our many trips to the phone booth. I figured she had enough problems and reasons to cry.

Then there were the late nights when Carly came stumbling in long past the time she told the babysitter she would. She always paid for the extra time, but there were tense words and the girl would threaten not to come again. Carly would cajole the babysitter until she agreed to give us another chance. But Carly would invariably come in late again. Once she didn't come home until the next morning. The fed-up babysitter decided to leave around midnight. She made sure I had brushed my teeth and gotten into my nightgown. She checked the stove and the locks on the windows. She gave me a hug and waited on the other side of the door to listen to me turn the locks. She called from a payphone when she got downstairs and made me promise to stay in my mother's bed with the TV on until she came home.

The performances didn't suffer right away. Carly kept getting good reviews, the audiences continued to give her standing ovations, and they continued to bring flowers. But sometimes she forgot to drop the checks she'd prepared in the mail and would come home from the supermarket with four boxes of cereal and no milk. When my school called about my tuition still being outstanding, I started opening the mail that was piling up on the dining room table. The bills were easy to recognize, I put those into stacks and spread the other envelopes out so she could see the senders names clearly.

Eventually, the reviews did change. Grandma Hélène would call about some blurb in a magazine and ask what "disjointed" and "phoned in" meant. She kept asking if we were all right, first in English then in French as if *"Est-ce que ça va?"* would give her a response that made her more comfortable. Carly would mumble something about a fight with the director, or a problem with wardrobe, or something else that was incomprehensible, but everything was always *la dee dah* in the end. She'd rush her off the phone with a promise to take her to a nice dinner that she never kept.

One night, Carly came to my room in her pajamas and leaned in the doorway. Her hair was rumpled and pressed to one side from the pillow, but her face was stage ready.

"Hey. Wanna do something fun?"

I put down my Anne of Green Gables and stared up from under my covers. My heart started pounding because the spark in her smile told me that whatever we were going to do would be a thrill. But then there was a trace of worry because I also knew there was a certain weirdness to this fun that I couldn't put my finger on. I jumped up and followed her to her closet where she layered me in a cloche hat, silk scarves, glittering necklaces and dangling earrings. We ran through scenes for half an hour, then went to eat at the diner around the corner, just as we were. The other patrons kept staring and we heard them whispering from the booths around us, but we didn't care. We kept our eyes on each other and tried not to laugh. When we came home a few hours later, an assistant from the theater was waiting in the lobby. Carly had blown off her rehearsal and this girl was charged first with finding out if she was all right, then with informing her that the understudy would be filling in for her from then on while she dealt with her "problem."

During Carly's involuntary hiatus, we lounged in front of the television in her room at night and she came in carrying plates arranged with celery sticks garnished alternately with peanut butter and mayonnaise. She'd waltz around the room holding the tray above her shoulder like a waiter at a fancy restaurant and settled on the bed with me to watch Charlton Heston part the Red Sea. We had watched *The Ten Commandments* every year around Easter time and knew every line. We mimicked Yul Bynner and his bowlegged stride and piercing stare. We giggled at how he managed to look like a giant in each of his scenes even though he was really a tiny little man in a gold cape. I stole glances at Carly and caught her eyes blinking slowly between Moses' monologues. I wanted to ask her why I was stuck with babysitters all the time. She stayed out late a lot and I knew she wasn't at the theater. I wondered about all the people buying tickets and sitting in the velvet seats waiting for the lights to dim and finding that it was someone else walking out into the spotlight instead of Carly. Wouldn't they be able to tell? Wouldn't they miss her? Wouldn't they ask for their money back and demand to see the thrilling Mathilda Séjour set fire to the stage? Would they write letters and picket in front of the theater and find their way to our apartment building and serenade in the lobby asking her to come back? Beg her to return to the stage and fill the room with the magic that broke their hearts and filled them with rapture at the same time?

No one came. The weeks rolled by and no one even called. I wanted to ask why, but I was afraid to shake her mood with questions. I already saw a strange sadness settling in her eyes and on the edges of her smiles and I wanted to erase it. So I smiled along with her and danced and pretended that our celery sticks and peanut butter were the most wonderful hors d'oeuvres I had ever tasted.

❧

It was still dark outside when I woke up suddenly. The hall light was on and I could hear my mother's footsteps. I sat up with a familiar dread shifting in my stomach. She hurried past my doorway and into the bathroom. She had the look of a fugitive, someone quietly afraid, preparing to flee. My school uniform was hanging on the doorknob of the closet.

"*Manmi*, what are you doing?"
Carly dashed into the room, startled to find me awake. The twitch of her lips as she gnawed at the insides of her mouth was desperate.

"Shhh, get up. We have to get dressed. Let's go."

"But, it's so early. What are you doing?"

"Shhhh... Listen to me, do what I tell you. Hurry up and get dressed."

I began to pout, as though acting more childish would force an explanation. I shuffled towards the bathroom and turned on the tub faucet.

"*Non, non*, we don't have time. There's no time for a bath. Just do your *toilette-de-bas* and brush your teeth. We have to go."
She was folding little bits of paper and stuffing them into her purse. Now and then she'd mumble something and shake her head and I'd think she was talking to me, but she wouldn't respond when I asked her to repeat her words. She darted from the kitchen to a closet down the hall. Its shelves were lined tightly with rows of library books, textbooks, poetry books, French, Spanish, Portuguese books.

Books she had pored over and studied for years, books that she valued as gold were flying from her hands into a garbage bag.

"*Manmi*, what are you doing? Are you throwing them away?"

"Shhhh, don't talk!" she whispered, panic-stricken. "Hurry up. Don't say anything…"

She dragged the garbage bag out to the compactor chute then hurried us down the stairs and out of the building. She had started avoiding elevators whenever possible and made us walk most places. That morning, in the wee hours, she took us to a diner where she sat straight-backed on her stool sipping sweet black coffee. I stared at my plate of scrambled eggs and buttered toast. The cheese was the same color as the plate and the milk wasn't cold. I didn't say a word. I thought that if I just stayed quiet, I could keep the crazed look in her eyes from igniting and setting the whole place on fire. I took tentative bites and watched the sun come up through the glass storefront.

We got to the steps of my school and waited an hour for the custodian to arrive and another thirty minutes before the principal's secretary, who always came in early, showed up. She looked at us like we were crazy. My mother mumbled something about having an early appointment in the city that couldn't be rescheduled. The secretary said I could sit in the office with her until my teacher came in. We watched my mother hurry off, gathering the lapels of her blazer into her chest. I watched her, feeling like I didn't recognize her anymore.

❧

My first communion was one of our final good days. I think the image of me wearing a lace headpiece with my crooked, gap-toothed smile sealed itself into her memory and from there, I would never grow up. My hair was freshly relaxed and styled into big rolling curls that framed my face like a doll. It was the first time that I remember being dressed all in white. My dress had short puffed sleeves with ruffles at the neck and hem, and a simple satin ribbon around the waist. My shoes were patent leather with lacy white tights. Carly wore dark blue pumps, a lavender patterned skirt with a coordinating silk blouse and navy blazer. It was a conservative look, but for drama she added a wide brimmed lavender hat with a neat veil pulled down to her chin. Grandma Hélène thought it was too much, but I love that it set her apart from all the other moms who wore belted polyester dresses, open-toed sandals, and fake pearls.

My father and his wife, Aurora, came to watch me receive the body and blood of Christ and said their goodbyes after taking a few pictures with me on the church steps. There was a small reception at Grandma Hélène's apartment. Aunt Marie Lourdes was in town with her husband and two boys, Aunt Madeleine was up from Miami, and there were some other adults, friends of the family, but no other kids. Someone brought platters of flaky patties filled with savory beef, chicken, and fish. Someone else brought a huge pot of *bouillon*, the most delicious Haitian stew that combined beef, yams, dumplings, spinach, carrots, and a broth that could celebrate joy, cure sickness, and erase bad memories. Everything was arranged elegantly on the round dining table on a white lace tablecloth, the one Grandma Hélène saved for high company and special occasions. There was good music playing, Tabou Combo, Skah Shah, and DP Express, as people sat on the plastic-covered sofas eating and drinking. There was a gigantic cake with impossibly sweet pink and white frosting that everybody raved about. I ran around with my cousins and danced until my smooth curls swelled into a huge frazzled mass. Of all the gifts I got that day—books, clothes, and cash—I cherished the gift from my Aunt Marie Lourdes most of all. It was a little gold pendant shaped in an oval and embossed with the figure of Our Lady of Lourdes, healer, patron saint of bodily ills. It was an obvious gift to give for a first communion, but I remember thinking that Carly needed it more than I did.

When the wretched years came, Carly put that day and that eight-year-old version of me in a tightly woven basket she had made when she still had a trace of strength left. In a compartment of her heart, she sat on the quiet bank of a river in the early morning someplace where the rising sun was peeking through tall trees. The air stayed still, making her feel light and clean. She knelt in the smooth pebbles and spread out blankets, lengths of leather cord, and bamboo. While the sun climbed, she worked for hours looping and tightening thick plaits around the bamboo until she had made a vessel strong enough to hide me away in.

❦

When I was ten, Carly took up with a man named C… I hated him from the moment I saw him, but I kept quiet about it for her sake. He was chubby and greasy with a receding hairline and dirty fingernails. He would offer me soda and candy, things that maybe most kids would have grabbed for, but I was not most kids. I had the ability to smell that wet vermin and the stench immediately made me want to vomit.

He told my mother something about how he was in the military in Germany and had been an officer in the *Landespolizei* in Berlin before moving to the United States. What he actually did for a living was never quite clear, but she was impressed with his stories about chasing down riff raff in the *Deutsche gassen*. In the summer he took us to Coney Island to ride on the rollercoasters and eat hot dogs with mustard and sauerkraut, which I hated. I took the cotton candy, but I refused to go on any rides with him. The only ride I did go on was the teacups with my mother. I only enjoyed it because it was just the two of us and he could only watch us from the sidelines.

When we walked together, I made sure I was never between them. I didn't want anyone to think that I was his child and I was certainly not going to hold his hand. I had left it hanging when Carly first introduced him to me. She apologized for my rudeness and explained that I was a bit shy with new people, which couldn't be further from the truth since I was the daughter of a Broadway actress. It didn't matter, though. She could have explained my behavior any way she wanted, it made no difference. I could tell that she didn't see him for what he was, so it would be up to me to keep the watch for her. But how strong is a child's will? He was monstrous and I was small. He put a spell on her and she couldn't hear my voice anymore. I didn't realize it then, but she had already given herself over and there was nothing I or anyone else could have done.

I waited up for her most nights. I did my homework in front of the television and nibbled on whatever I could scavenge from our cupboards and the fridge. I turned canned salmon, plum tomatoes, goat cheese, and Melba toast into fancy bites that I arranged on a plate and ate with my pinky pointed up. I mixed orange and cranberry juice in a highball glass, dropped green grapes in the bottom and pretended I was in a television commercial for some fancy drink. I twirled and swayed in one of her nightgowns in front of the nightlight in the kitchen and made dancing shadows until I was tired. I settled in my bed with a book but could never fall sleep until I heard her stumble in. Sometimes she wandered into my room and passed out next to me on my twin bed. When I cuddled against her I could smell the ugliness of where she'd been. No amount of Jean Naté or First from Van Cleef and Arpels could cover the odor of cigarettes and alcohol steeping in her hair. And there was another odor, one that clung to her skin and it filled my throat with a taste of metal and rotting meat. I don't remember when it became the routine for me to creep to the bathroom for a warm rag to wipe her face and neck before pulling my sheets over us.

She was officially cut from the show. Almost a year went by and after so munch spending and ignoring of actual bills, we had to leave our nice apartment. Grandma Hélène wanted us to come back to her, but Carly wouldn't do it. Instead we moved in with an actress friend and we played the bohemian mother and child living the artsy life. We visited Grandma Hélène from time to time but never stayed long.

"Are you hungry? I have soup I made last night, and some good bread from the Haitian bakery. You want?"

We would sit at the table like refugees quietly accepting alms from a compassionate stranger.

"You want to watch television, Ollie? Let me see what they are giving now. What time is it?"
Grandma Hélène turned the television knob around and around looking for a kid show for me, or at least something with a laugh track to fill the air with something other than our spoons clinking against

the bowls. When we were almost finished eating and had glasses of fruit punch in front of us, Grandma Hélène couldn't stay quiet anymore.

"Mathilda, what is that color you have in your hair? Did you do that to yourself?"

That was our cue to leave. Carly put her glass down and wiped my mouth with her napkin. She made a big deal of brushing crumbs off my shirt and smoothing my hair before gathering up our things to go.

"Mathilda, what are you doing? She's not finished yet! I have cake..."

"Olive, let's go. We're going."

Carly guided my arms into my jacket sleeves as if I were a toddler and couldn't do it myself. She checked to make sure my sneakers were tied then hoisted her heavy tote bag onto her shoulder. She hurried us out before Grandma Hélène could say too much more.

She called on her theater pals who still idolized her even though their looks were now more full of pity than awe, and we went from basement to attic, front room to back room, crashing with different people for weeks at a time. I'd come in from school and find her waiting for me by the door with an apple or a banana. To keep my strength up, she'd say. We'd huddle together at night with no real plans and no money, but we were all right because I was her talisman. She kissed me all over my face before turning out the lights every night, but I couldn't keep my eyes closed. I turned my child's will into steel and chose to sleep less. I got used to the sound of the leaky bathtub faucet, the fluttering rise and fall of someone masturbating in the next room, the zip of a lighter as someone lit a candle or a joint to ease into things I couldn't possibly imagine. I stopped being hungry and chose to do fine with a slice of bread with canned sardines and some milk. I was hardly ever sick and focused all my energy on wrapping my mother in my force field. I thought it worked for a while, that I really did protect her. I didn't bother her with doing my hair or washing my clothes. A ponytail was easy with a hard bristle brush and a bubble tie, and I scrubbed my panties by hand in the bathroom sink with a bar of Ivory soap. I didn't mention the hole in the sole of the shoes I wore to school every day. None of it mattered. I willed those things away to focus on keeping my Carly safe.

But as it turns out, a child's will is not enough. There were hurts that I simply couldn't mend, and turbulences in my mother's head that I couldn't possibly name. C… had been feeding her a steady supply of different drugs and small amounts of cash to buy food and toiletries. She had waded into his muddy world and visited rooms at addresses far from anything a sheltered Colonel's daughter would ever know. His thin smile and slithery words worked well on her weakened psyche; he must have understood right away that here was one he could use. And he did.

He fed her the poison and even though it made her sick, he promised that if she just took a little more it would make her well. So she got sicker and weaker. Sicker and stranger. Sicker and more lost. Sicker and more desperate. Sicker, then well again. Sicker, then light as a feather, then floating like an angel. Every time she came into contact with him she seemed to change into a zombie, but he had the power to make her feel better again. After months of free rides, the time had come for her to start paying for her trips to heaven and he knew exactly what price to set. When she was high enough, a room was set up with lights, a mattress, and a camera.

The men came in, sometimes by twos, for hours. There was clean up, makeup, and costume changes in between. He coached her on angles and tone and speed, and money shots. More cameras came in. There were drinks in paper cups to wash down the sour taste of the men and to keep the languid glaze in her eyes. The first time, she hovered above consciousness and C... convinced her that everything would work out fine.

By the fourth or fifth time, there were set changes, props, other women, and no room for protest. Carly had no other way to make money and she was completely dependent on what he gave her. She needed the drugs even though they were killing her, and her body wouldn't move forward without them. Her sober moments were scattered and spread thin over the days, and while I was at school she agreed to practically anything he suggested. One night when I was curled up under the covers in the twin bed we shared, hiding from the smell of whatever they were smoking in the next room, he asked.

It was the end of a long day of shooting and they had come back to sprawl in the living room of the musty apartment where we were staying at the time like exhausted rats. The television was on low, my mother was bleary-eyed and wasted, and he asked. He nudged her, saying that he could give me something to relax first, so I wouldn't feel much. He said he had done it before, with his own son, and that the boy didn't even remember it afterwards. He reminded her that she owed him, and she knew it. Her heartbeat reverberated in her throat. She blinked slowly and looked toward the door separating me from the breath of ruin.

I was usually nervous about being fully undressed and hadn't taken a real bath in days. I mostly freshened up with a washcloth and quick in case somebody banged on the bathroom door saying they didn't mind if I stayed while they peed. I used Carly's deodorant even though there was no hair under my arms yet. My fingernails always came back with a faint black line under them when I scratched behind my ears, but to her I was still clean. When we'd curl together in our too-small space, she held me tight and breathed me in like I was her last clean thing.

There was no other choice. My mother was utterly helpless and she could hear no one but him. He asked one more time, and in one of her last moments of clarity, her answer rolled up like oil over her tongue and pushed slowly through her teeth.

"No."

She couldn't save herself; that much she knew, so she put me in the basket and pushed me down the river toward the unknown. She waded into the tall grass along the water's edge and watched me drift away. She closed her eyes and was gone, gone, gone.

Within twenty-four hours I was sitting in a bubble bath in a clean tub with a faucet that did not leak. Carly had waited until I was asleep and asked one of her friends, one of those that actually cared about her, to carry me to Grandma Hélène's house. I don't remember leaving the apartment, getting into a car, or being handed off to my grandmother's arms when we reached her door. I only remember waking up in her soft bed and seeing her yellow silk drapes pulled neatly aside to let the light in. Her dresser had a glass vanity set arranged with powders and perfumes, and the cushy down comforter was a blue and yellow floral pattern. I opened my eyes and saw her smiling at me with a tray of scrambled eggs, avocado and toast in her hands. Her face was controlled and tilted in her usual way. She set the tray on the night table and sat next to me.

"Eat some breakfast, Olive *chérie*. You need your strength."

I wanted to ask her why I was there and where my mother was, but the way she avoided my eyes and stared off at the window, I knew I wouldn't get a real answer. I looked around at the pristine room with the pressed dust ruffle and frosted sconces. I sat up and the blue rug at the foot of the bed looked like water swirling under my dangling toes. I wanted to tell Grandma about the flaked paint around the windowsill of the room I slept in just the night before. I wanted to talk about the smell of ylang ylang, stale underarm and week-old panties in the closet where we crammed all our stuff. On top of that the smell of marijuana hung over everything else. I wanted to say that there were bunches of glittery tank tops and ripped fishnet stockings in our dresser, and peep toe heels stuffed under our bed. I wanted to talk about how much I wanted to slice myself open to find the remains of the child I hardly remembered being. I worried that new language would hurt her, terrify her, so I said nothing. Grandma slowly brought forkfuls of eggs to my mouth cupping her other hand under my chin. As I looked into her eyes, I imagined Carly weeping as she watched me float away on the river's current, knowing that we would never be together again.

☙❧

The next time I laid eyes on her, it was a strange reunion. Our severing had left a terrible gash that eventually scabbed over, but all it took was a little pressure for it to throb and ooze all over again. The hole her absence left in my middle was being filled with Aunt Marie Lourdes. I was fourteen and forgetting how much I needed my own mother. Aunt Marie Lourdes was bread and comfort, and she was uncertainty. Marie Lourdes was fresh herbs, and she was delirium. Marie Lourdes was vegetable gardens in moist black earth, and she was feeling my way blindly through a wasteland. Only two days before she arrived, Aunt Marie Lourdes and Uncle Aaron told me they had found my mother and that they arranged for her to be brought home to us. I didn't know what to say, so I said nothing.

I woke up early and that whole morning anticipation rolled around in the pit of my stomach with the weight of a bowling ball that couldn't make it to the end of the lane to crash into the pins. I roamed the house, antsy, but not joyous. I squatted in the yard trying to count the different vegetables and herbs we grew but kept losing my place. Each time I got to the mimosa bush sitting under the apple and pear trees, I got lost and started over. It was while I was running my finger along those fanned out leaves and watching them fold in from my touch that I heard a car door shut in the driveway. I ran through the kitchen and up to my bedroom to peek out the window but only caught the top of Uncle Aaron's head moving towards the front door. I crept slowly to the hall and back down the stairs, sliding along the wall, waiting for someone to call me. I was almost at the bottom, still out of view when I heard his voice.

"I know you're there, honey. Come on out and see your mother."

I was suddenly dizzy and I had to open my mouth to breathe before stepping down onto the landing. She had on huge dark sunglasses so I couldn't tell if she was looking at me or not. After four years of her being missing, I wondered where they had found her. From the yellow knit mini-dress with long sleeves and black knee-high boots that were way too heavy for July, it couldn't have been anyplace nice. Her hair was short and badly damaged from processing and coloring. She had a beige zebra print tote bag tucked under one arm and with her free hand she kept touching the back of her head, smoothing it. I couldn't take my eyes off her.

Uncle Aaron reached for me and when I inched forward she grabbed me with an urgency that made me uncomfortable. With her face against mine for that brief moment, I heard her give a nervous chuckle. It was like she was in a rush and I was an adoring fan that she was happy to see but couldn't talk to and needed to get away from quickly. She wrapped her arm around my shoulder and squeezed me to her for an instant, but before I could breathe her in she let me go and followed Uncle Aaron into the kitchen. I stood in the hallway, waiting for trumpets and violins, or a choir to swell behind the tears that usually accompany this kind of scene in the movies. But there was only the sliding of chairs, pouring of coffee, then the clinking of teaspoons against cups. A breeze from the back door blew through the curtains and tossed some paper towels from the counter. I crept in to pick them up and squatted in a corner under a hanging plant to stare at this woman I had missed but didn't know anymore.

There was a plate of soft cheese and a baguette torn into pieces, a bowl of blueberries on the table, and a pot of thick yellow soup on the stove waiting for her. It was the New Year's kind but it also popped up at funerals or whenever there was a need for comfort. Everyone had their own spin on it. Some people liked it with noodles, other people liked potatoes better. Marie Lourdes didn't know what shape she would find her sister in, so she had fortified hers with watercress and spinach. The chopped up carrots and yams gave to the slightest push of the tongue against the palate. The chunks of seasoned beef slid right off the bone and she kept the dumplings small. She remembered her sister fishing for them in her bowl when they were young; they had always been her favorite.

That day my mother only wanted some sweet coffee. She held her cup with both hands and sat with her legs crossed at the ankles and her knees pressed together like a prim Catholic schoolgirl. Her shoulders hunched forward as though she were whispering secrets to her coffee instead of drinking it. She rocked back and forth and wiped the steam that gathered on the tip of her nose. Uncle Aaron put on a classical record and hummed along with the violins and trumpets. Aunt Marie Lourdes pulled the blinds all the way open to show her sister the garden in the yard. No one said anything about the tears that slid down her cheeks from behind the sunglasses she kept adjusting on her face.

After my mother finally agreed to have a piece of bread and a bit of soup, I followed as Aunt Marie Lourdes led her up to my room. There was a mattress on the floor prepared with all of my stuffed animals arranged like an audience to welcome her. She whispered that she was tired and slid onto the neat sheets. I watched her fall asleep within seconds of her cheek pressing against the cool pillow, fully dressed, sunglasses still on. Aunt Marie Lourdes removed them while I knelt at the edge of the mattress. I pulled off my mother's boots and looked at her feet. I could see through her torn stockings that they were badly callused and her toenails were overgrown. I propped her feet in my lap and cupped her heels with my palms. I wanted to weep for how broken and dirty she was. I wanted my tears to flow out and wash her feet and make them new again. But they wouldn't come.

When she woke up hours later, Aunt Marie Lourdes took her sister into the bathroom and undressed her like a baby. I stood at her side as handmaiden. We put every bit of her clothing into a garbage bag and helped her step into the tub. We spent more than an hour washing her hair and scrubbing her down under the hard spray of the shower, then we filled the tub so she could soak. With our sleeves rolled up and our necks sweaty, we soaped her body all over again with steady pressure, and she never flinched. During the bath, Marie Lourdes knelt along the middle of the tub with one foot in the water and leaned her sister against her knee. She poured water over her head and held her like a child. I stayed at the ready with more bath oil or soap or towels. The room was quiet except for the sound of the water tumbling from a cup over my mother's head. We waited for her to say something, moan, anything. But she made no sound at all. Her eyes were mostly blank, but there were moments when an open sadness came through her stare and her whole face seemed to be on the verge of crumbling. I looked hard into her eyes, trying to hear what she would say, but nothing came through. When my mother was finally clean and toweled off, I lifted a fresh bathrobe as Aunt Marie Lourdes guided her out of the tub and I helped rub cocoa butter on her bare skin. We dressed her in new underwear and plain white pajamas. She sat on the floor while Aunt Marie Lourdes massaged peppermint oil into her scalp and brushed the uneven remnants of her hair from front to back and wrapped it all in a silk scarf.

She would have looked after her sister as she had when they were just girls. She would have introduced her to gardening and long strolls through their suburban neighborhood on the North Shore. Winters were hard, but the house was warm and she knew how to make the dense breakfast rolls the cook used to serve for breakfast in Haiti. She would have made them for her every day. She would have brewed teas and mixed oils and used her healing hands to soothe the spirits that were not satisfied with just dancing, but had torn and smashed their way through her sister's head. But quickly, not even a full month after arriving, Carly found her way downtown to the shadowy corners of Rue St. Denis at night and into the hands of those who could feed those dancing, smashing spirits. She gathered her zebra-print bag and crept out of the house when no one was home and disappeared. Marie Lourdes never saw her sister alive again.

༄ঞ

When I was grown and had slain my own monsters, I found her living in a group home in Brooklyn. I wanted to move her in with me in the West Village apartment I had at the time, with a visiting nurse and all the books and music she wanted. She could even smoke her cigarettes in the communal garden in the back, but she wouldn't come. She insisted that she was fine and didn't want to leave where she was.

So I was dutiful and I visited. I steeled myself against the need for a mother and went through the motions with a phantom. This is what I believed, what I told myself every time I walked up the desolate block on Bergen Street. I came in with my brow furrowed, neck and shoulders braced against

the artificial plants in the lobby, the industrial
ammonia smell in the hallways, the vending
machines full of chips and soda. I held my purse
with the strap across my chest and squeezed it
against my stomach like those old white ladies who
fret when they see a young black man walking in
their direction in the street. There was no threat in
this place. These were quiet rheumy women and
men who mumbled to themselves, smoked too
much, and shuffled from the game room to the TV
room to the cafeteria to the pay phone in the
hallway. I wore combat boots and stepped
cautiously on the gray and white linoleum, avoiding
making any more noise than I had to. If I had to use
the bathroom, I held it in. Going into one of the
common lavatories was uncomfortable enough, but
it would have been worse to relieve myself in that
place where I couldn't possibly feel relief. Despite
the smiling staff wearing nubby sweaters, rubber
clogs, and pens in their hair, there was no comfort
there, only worn souls with entire lives floating by
under a bridge where other people were peering
down, trying to remember what was lost.

I brought her sweet coffee from the deli on the
corner and sat on her rumpled bed while she
rambled. Her words were mostly disconnected and
didn't make much sense; song lyrics and poems

with my name laced through them. Sometimes, though, her words threaded together into stories I wished I could un-hear. It was one thing to overhear Grandma Hélène whining on the phone to Aunt Madeleine, or to eavesdrop on conversations between Aunt Marie Lourdes and Uncle Aaron after they thought I was asleep, but hearing the history pour out of my mother's own mouth was hard to take. I couldn't tell what I could believe, which stories were imagined by her chopped up mind and which were horrifyingly true. I looked into her face and it was a shadow that looked back at me. Her skin had turned ashy and she moved like she wasn't sure she was really there. When I responded to her words, she looked surprised that I had heard them in the first place. The longer I was there, the more life drained out of me. So I'd leave quickly, quietly, sometimes in tears.

Carly was finally able to move into a government-sponsored apartment where a social worker visited her twice a month and a nurse came once a week. She collected dozens of bottles of knock-off perfumes and body lotions that she rarely used. She just lined them up on her bathroom shelf and made sure to show me that they were there whenever I came over. I bought a nail kit and gave her manicures and pedicures from time to time. I used lotion from one of her many bottles and she always wanted red nail polish, so I stopped bothering to bring any other colors. She spent the government money she received every month on costume jewelry, trinkets, and handbags from the Korean gift shop around the corner. She got scarves, belt, hats of all kinds, and dozens of cheap wigs. She stuffed most of what she bought into her drawers and piled it onto her dresser, but the wigs were another story. She kept them brushed and styled on the backs of chairs, on doorknobs. When she was tired of one, or couldn't find a proper place to display it, she just threw it away. Her own hair was irreversibly damaged and had fallen out in ragged patches over the years. She wore the wigs to cover what she wanted to hide but also to show what was still there. I never knew which character would greet me when I knocked on her door. A honey brown Farrah Fawcett might feather just past her shoulders, or a sleek, black bob might cut right at her jawbone. She'd cross her legs and sit at the foot of her bed gazing at the perpetually turned-on television. She stalked the PBS channel for old black and white movies and when a scene came on that stirred a certain memory, her flat stare would turn to longing. I massaged the twitch in her brow that fluttered uncontrollably and gently squeezed her cheeks when I caught her grinding her teeth. She looked down and let me rub her face, but the twitch didn't go away. My healing powers were long gone.

On one of my last visits, I scrolled through the music list on my phone for something to play while I prepared a shrimp salad in her tiny kitchen. I found "Los Hermanos" by Mercedes Sosa and put it on repeat. As the guitar line floated through the closed air of her room, she became like a baby turning instinctively towards the voice of its mother. Her face lifted with soft excitement as she sang along, swaying and remembering every word, in Spanish. When it was over, just before it started up again, she looked at me with a gratitude that broke my heart.

❧❦

I found her whispering her last breaths on an early morning in fall. I knocked on her door for a whole minute with no answer and I knew. I leaned my forehead on the cool metal, listening to the sound of the television that she always left on. I finally fished in my bag for my key and went in. The brown and gold curtains were still drawn, most likely from the night before. As I stepped in further

I smelled old coffee and I could hear the bathroom faucet that dripped when the hot knob wasn't turned tight enough. She was in her bed, fully dressed, wearing a short blonde wig. There was a bowl of soggy cereal on the nightstand with the spoon swimming in it. I moved without panic and sat next to her. I gathered the last pieces of Carly in my arms and there was nothing left to do but wait. I slid off her wig and pressed my cheek against hers and listened as she murmured things she had already said, names of characters, titles of books, things she could say only to me and get a response of 'Yes, I know'. When I felt her go, I rocked her shoulders, now heavy with release, and whispered her given name: Mathilda Séjour.

I wanted to call my Aunt Marie Lourdes, but there was still too much hurt between us for me to dial her number and risk falling apart at the sound of her voice. I wanted to call my grandmother, but I was afraid of her having some kind of attack if I gave her the news over the phone. I called Aunt Madeleine in Miami and told her that her baby sister was gone. I know it hit her like the falling bricks we had been expecting all along, but she stayed as solid as I needed her to be. She said she'd come up, she had questions and suggestions about what to do, but it was my job to take care of Carly. It had always been. She didn't have a will or any final instructions, so I made all the decisions. It took some doing, but after a small service in Brooklyn, I sent her remains with Grandma Hélène to be buried in Haiti. I told her she could have whatever ceremony she wanted down there because I had already said my goodbye. The family mausoleum in Jacmel's countryside was made to expand, and I knew that Margo, wherever she was, would welcome her youngest grandchild with cradling arms. My only request was that Grandma Hélène put in a red pipe before they sealed   the   grave.

4 Aurora

Aurora loved to braid my hair. I usually ended up sitting between her knees with a comb and a jar of Ultra Sheen when I came to spend the weekend. Her hands were soft but she had the firm touch needed for tight cornrows. She pulled and parted my hair, dipped her fingers into the pomade and traced her comb over my scalp like she was carving roads through uncharted earth. We'd be in the parlor in the afternoons in summer with a breeze from the bay windows blowing through the jungle on my head. She'd play Roberta Flack and Stevie Wonder records or put in a movie rental to keep me from getting antsy. She always made fresh treats and I never had to reach too far to put my hands on a cookie or a brownie. When she was finished, her complicated styles looked like mazes. I ran my fingers over the lines trying to discover which braid was tied to which path. When I looked in the mirror, I saw another version of my eyes, nose, and mouth looking back at me. My face was the same, but with the magic in her hands she had made me into a new girl.

"You like it, don't you, honey?"

My answer was stuck in my throat. I whirled around and wrapped my arms around her waist and pressed my face into her bosom.

"Aww, what's the matter, sugar? You all right?"
Her voice undulated like warm gusts of air. It swirled around my ears and made everything that was ever bitter turn sweet. Those couple of Sunday nights a month always came too soon and I never wanted to go back to the routine of Carly's madness. When I was with Aurora, I could be languid and blank. She thought of everything I could want, like painting our nails with glitter nail polish, or practicing cartwheels in the narrow backyard with her two nieces. When they came over, the three of us gobbled grilled cheese sandwiches, green grapes, and Pepsi until I thought

my stomach would burst. And there were always homemade chocolate chip cookies. I used to chew around the crispy edges until I found a chip and let it melt in my mouth or get stuck between my teeth. The bittersweet taste seeped into my tongue with warning, but I kept biting into the cookie and enjoyed the temporary bliss.

During the week, when I was home with Carly, I was sharp as a hawk. I waited for her to fall asleep before starting on my homework at the kitchen counter and kept an ear out for her sleepy mumbling or shuffling footsteps to the bathroom. I knew how to be ready with a cup of ginger ale or ice water and saltines to soothe her stomach, or a cold rag to calm her nervous sweats. I knew which songs to sing, and at what volume, to make her quiet down and maybe even join me. Aurora didn't need my songs. She was perfect.

My father worked so much that he even went in to the office for a few hours on weekends. There were so many meetings to sit through and reports to prepare and he could never walk away until every item was checked off his list. On Friday nights, Aurora would save a plate for him in the oven and go to heat it when she heard his key in the door. She watched TV in the parlor waiting up for him so much that after a while there was a permanent indentation from her left shoulder and hip in the leather couch. Most of the time when she opened her eyes, she caught the end of some caper Ralph Kramden and Ed Norton had gotten into in their black and white, one-room world. She liked the physical comedy that was so easily expressed with Ralph's bulging eyes or Norton's exaggerated double takes or Alice's deadpan sighs.

One Friday night, at the sound of the key, Aurora straightened her silk nightgown with matching robe and fluffed her hair, still arranged in the soft curls she had styled that morning. She took the travel sized Trésor she kept in the candy dish and spritzed her bosom and behind her neck before hurrying down the stairs to greet her husband. He set his leather briefcase on the foyer bench, and their routine was for her to take his jacket and rub his back as they walked down the hall. The kitchen was lit only by the fluorescent clock on the stove and a white candle on the table. He sat down heavily and waited for her to serve him.

"Smothered chops. Haven't had that in a while, huh?" she asked.

He nodded with a thin smile and loosened his tie. He opened up his napkin and took a few sips from the glass of water that was sweating onto the tablecloth. Aurora prepared a much smaller plate for herself and took a seat across from him.

"Thank you, Rorie," he said, and bent his head to start eating. The heaviness of the day rolled off his shoulders as soon as the first forkful of potato salad settled in his mouth. He had not tasted gherkin pickles until he met Aurora. He had never had any pickles at all. Coming from the cooking world of his mother and sisters, he thought he knew food, and women for that matter. But Aurora gave him something totally new. She was the match he should have made the first time around. She fit him in a way he recognized but could have never articulated in his own thoughts. She was the last of four heiresses to a farm equipment fortune in Georgia. She played the piano and was a pink and green sorority girl. She was the kind of woman who was bred for marriage in a way that made her husband believe that there was nothing else in the world any woman would ever want.

When they met she was a first grade teacher at a private school on the Upper West Side. She was quiet and ladylike, but her curves couldn't help but draw the eyes of men and the arms of every student in her class at the end of each day. Though there wasn't an ounce on Aurora that didn't belong there, after they were married she liked to tease her new husband that her waist was bigger than his. *"Baby, we gon' have to put some meat up on you!"* She came from a place where a man's crisp white shirt wrapped tight around a sizeable belly was a good thing. Never mind about high cholesterol, hypertension, and heart disease, or whatever else might be lurking in those heavy bowels. Big Daddy was supposed to be BIG. It meant he was successful enough to have anything he wanted to eat, and that he could intimidate when he stepped into a room without saying a word. Over time, Aurora remedied her husband's lank with the lessons she had learned back when she stood on a chair in her mother's kitchen to see inside the pots on the stove.

Besides honey glazed ham and saucy ribs, creamy macaroni and cheese, mustard greens with thick hocks bathing in pot liquor, and every other typical southern dish on record, Aurora was also good at Italian and French cuisine. Everyone went wild for her Boeuf Bourguignon, and her stuffed peppers were in demand at every family party. But that night Samuel couldn't finish his meal down to the last scrape like usual, and he only took one bite from the slice of chilled lemon meringue pie she slid in front of him afterwards.

As he wiped his mouth and took a sip of water, something pitched in the silence, something invisible, but with the force of a hurricane. Aurora blinked slowly and took a deep breath, but my father spoke first.

"Rorie, I have something to tell you."

She leaned in on her elbows and twirled one of her dangling earrings like it was a lock of hair. Her lips parted slightly without sound.

"Something has happened to Mathilda and Olive is at her grandmother's house. I'm going to pick her up tomorrow morning. She's going to stay with us from now on."

Storm clouds full of cutting rain and ripping winds passed over Aurora's eyes for a moment, only a moment. Then they were gone.

"I know this is a big change and it is asking a lot, but…"

"Samuel, I'm pregnant."

A phantom rush of air swirled in and sucked the breath right out of both their throats. The digital light from the stove cast a green tint on everything and made them look like they were going to vomit. Aurora quickly took his hands.

"I don't want you to worry about anything, honey. All right? Olive'll be with us, and everything's gonna be all right. You'll see. We're gonna be just fine. We're a family."

The next morning my father held my hand and led me through his big house on Hollow Road as if I hadn't been spending weekends there for three years already. He had to have read the confused look on my face, but he still insisted on performing what felt like some sort of ritual.

The house was a Victorian style with wooden front steps and a wide porch. The room that I slept in had plush peach carpet and the wallpaper was sprayed with tiny blue flowers capped with wood crown molding. The bathroom down the hall had a huge claw-footed tub and black and white mosaic tile on the floor. Dark wood paneling went halfway up the walls with more molding framing the ceilings in there and everywhere else throughout the house.

I followed him through each floor waiting for him to speak. I watched his double chin profile as he gestured to windows and random pieces of furniture. I nodded like I understood what he was trying to express. He gave a sort of smile here and there, but it always ended up looking like a grimace.

"You're happy to be here, Olive?"

"Yes, Papi."

"Good." He gave a quick corporate nod.

"You know you're going to be staying here with us, right?"

"Yes, but…"

"What is it?" I cleared my throat to make my voice bigger because I suddenly felt very small.

"What's Carly gonna to do without me?"

My father's eyebrows raised in a way that made his hairline pull away from his face. It was his turn to clear his throat.

"Is that what you call her?"

We stood there staring at each other, my heart in my mouth and sweat dripping down the back of his head, seeping into his starched white collar. He didn't answer my question and I didn't answer his. Finally, when the air between us became too heavy to breathe anymore, he changed the subject.

"Come. Aurora made lunch and the girls are coming over soon. Come."

I followed him downstairs just as Aurora's nieces, Jolene and Abigail, came through the door with a jump rope and a huge bag of candy for us to share.

"Hi Olive! Come on, let's go jump. You wanna turn?"

"Jo, we gotta eat first! Aunt Rorie made fried chicken!"

"I'm not hungry, I already had a bunch of these gummies."

"Girl, please! Candy don't count as food!"

The girls and I went out the back door to the yard and we ran around for a couple of hours. We ate the chicken and the thick fries Aurora prepared and washed it all down with cherry soda that had actual Maraschino cherries in the bottom of our glasses.

Weeks went by and I found myself slipping easily from my former life and into my new one. Aurora was in constant motion and was compelled to feed us along with her growing belly. I had fruit loops in the morning and stared with wide eyes while she sat down to a piece of cheesecake sprinkled with corn chips. After school, I came home to the smell of baked chicken and mashed potatoes that we enjoyed with freshly brewed iced tea. I did my homework at the kitchen table with a stack of coconut cookies Aurora somehow found time to bake. Actually, she had nothing but time. At six months my father encouraged her to take her maternity leave early. She knew that it most likely meant that she would not be going back to work at all. Her job had always been an opportunity to nurture children in a way she never thought she'd be able to, but now that she was having her own baby, giving it up seemed easy. She stayed home and pressed shirts. She dusted the furniture. She wiped down windows, and even scrubbed the bathroom floors. She was a ball full of not only baby, but of energy and she was determined to keep the whole house in spotless order without disturbing her curls or her smile.

As the weeks inched on, Aurora started having trouble falling asleep at night. She was almost eight months along but refused to use pregnancy as an excuse to sit and fan herself with a glass of iced tea. When the house couldn't get any cleaner, she started logging the meals she cooked into a cookbook diary she said she would use to teach me how to cook so I could take over when the baby came. In the dark, she listened to the silence on the other side of her husband's snoring and imagined what it was going to be like when the baby came to disrupt both. She couldn't wait for all the wailing and feeding and changing and constant rocking. Every now and then she heard me when I woke up gasping in the middle of the night in my room. During the day, I laughed and ate and even sang, but at night Carly haunted my dreams. She was always falling down an elevator shaft in slow motion and calling for me. Her face was a blur and she mouthed my name with no sound. Her voice slowly came circling around me like echoes then floated back down behind her as she fell into the darkness. I tried to catch her but stopped at the edge of her abyss, teetering, almost falling in after her. I'd wake up sweating with my body painfully tense, my shoulders crunched in fear.

Aurora would creep in sometimes with a mug of warm milk to chase away the bad dreams. I cuddled against her belly and listened for my little brother or sister until I drifted off. In the morning, the bad dream seemed far away. I stepped out of bed feeling like there had been a battle in the night and that I had come out the winner. I got dressed in front of the mirror and when I asked it who was the fairest of them all, it showed me Aurora's face time and time again. Was it any wonder that I thought I loved her more? I thought I could adapt to my new world and keep my mother alive in some deep shadowy section of my heart, but I was wrong. I wasn't a winner. I was a traitor.

᷍᷍

"Please, Rorie, let me stay up with you!"

"Naw, Ollie this baby is moving around too much. I'm not gonna be able to drag you upstairs once he settles down. Go on now."

"Wait, how do you know it's a boy?" I knelt at her feet and put my ear to her belly.

"Hello in there! Are you a boy or a girl? Kick once for boy and twice for girl!"

Aurora tickled the back of my neck and playfully swatted my behind.

"Girl, you better go on upstairs. Brush your teeth, wash your face and hands before you get in the bed. Go on now."

"All right, all right! Good night baby boy! Or girl!"

She stuck her tongue out at me as I went and she listened for the water turning on and off, then for the clicking of my bedroom lamp before easing off her slippers and stretching out on the sofa. On those nights, after tossing and using all the throw pillows to find a position the baby would accept, she'd end up drifting off long before Ralph and Norton even got started with their shenanigans. The key would turn and she wouldn't move. The front door would open and close and there was no one there to take my father's coat. He continued to the kitchen and the plate she'd prepared for him was still in the refrigerator covered in foil. After eating alone, he'd go up to the parlor and find her snoring, wedged into place with pillows. He'd continue up to bed without bothering to wake her up or turn off the television.

The larger Aurora's belly grew, the more distant my father became. He spent even more time at work and his conversations with his wife became shorter and shorter. Aurora stepped up her tried and true methods of charm. She started baking something different every day. That spring was hotter than usual and turned sweltering before even hitting the middle of May, but it was pecan pie on Mondays, rum cake with vanilla ice cream on Tuesdays, black currant cobbler on Wednesdays, chocolate chip cookies on Thursdays, and lemon meringue pie on Fridays. What we didn't finish eating, she gave me to take to school and share with my classmates. On the weekends it was fruit salad with fresh whipped cream. She went to the nail salon to do her feet once a week since she could no longer bend over to give herself a pedicure. She even started setting a timer to buzz right in the middle of the *Honeymooners* so that she'd be awake to waddle downstairs when my father came home. The lace-trimmed gowns and robes she usually wore didn't fit anymore so it was short cotton mumus, with matching slippers. It was so hot that her curls flattened and stuck to her neck even though she positioned the fan to blow directly at her without oscillating.

After supper one late night, my father settled next to Aurora on the sofa and loosened his tie. His belly was only about a month smaller than hers and he was constantly clearing his throat.

"How are you? It's getting close, isn't it?" he asked.

"Yeah, it should be another two weeks maybe. Doctor says I've been doing real good. With stayin' active and everything."

"Do you want to hire someone to help you in the house after?"

She smoothed the hair along her forehead and smiled before answering.

"No... No, honey, I think I'll be all right. No need for all that."

Early the next morning, just before the sun started peeking through the blinds, Aurora's water broke while she was still in bed. My father dropped me off at Grandma Hélène's on the way to the hospital. Thirteen hours later, there was a baby girl.

⌘

When I watched him hold my sister like a little football that might fumble at any moment, I wondered what my father had been like with me when I was that small. I wondered if he had ever dropped me or forgotten to change my diaper or let me cry until my face turned red. I wondered how often he had kissed me, nuzzled me into his neck to feel me wiggle and breathe, if he had ever paced back and forth with my head just below his chin, saying nonsense words in a small voice that he thought a baby might like.

Those thoughts disappeared as soon as he placed her my arms. She looked like a beige pod wrapped in a pink blanket. I stared into her new squinty face and swore that I saw a resemblance with mine. She was a warm weight that felt so natural against my chest and in the cook of my arm. I couldn't wait to talk to her, to teach her, and tell her all my secrets. Aurora named her Ashley.

She was born right at the end of the school year so I was home to be around her right from the start. I wanted be with her all the time, but she was too small to play with. All she did was sleep and eat and poop. She didn't even cry so much at first, but whenever she did I jumped up to see what faces and sounds I could make to make her quiet down. I waited for any opportunity to touch her, help change her, kiss her little feet, kiss any part of her that was uncovered. It was summer and we were home every day while my father was perpetually at work. Now that there was a baby, Aurora didn't have time to do my hair. I started making my own sandwiches and I got pretty good at a double-cornrow hairstyle that I thought made me look like Laura Ingalls. My father started sending his shirts out to be pressed and folded, and he was eating more Chinese food on his way home instead of looking in the fridge for the usual plate.

One day, Aurora asked me to watch Ashley while she took a shower. There wasn't much to it, obviously. She was only three months old and didn't do much but move her hands and feet a little when she wasn't sleeping. I turned on the TV and sat on the floor watching her blink, yawn, open and close her tiny hands. I waited until I heard the shower running for a while before I scooped her out of her baby seat and settled her into my arms. I cradled her securely, even supported her head the right way in the bend of my elbow. I pressed my lips to her forehead and breathed in her warm clean smell. I felt an overwhelming excitement and pride that she was mine, my own little person to adore. I started singing one of Carly's songs and put her name in it. *"Oui monsieur la petite Ashley, est tellement tellement jolie, dans le pays tous les garcons..."* I was so captivated by her face changing from surprise to smile to sleepy blink that I didn't notice when the shower turned off. Aurora appeared suddenly in front of us, wrapped in her towel. Her hair was wet, dripping onto her shoulders and down her back.

"You didn't ask permission to take the baby out of that chair, did you?"

Her voice was calm, but there was a twitch in her eyes. I looked up and straightened my shoulders so she could see that she had nothing to worry about because I was doing everything right. I held Ashley securely and stayed on the floor with my legs crossed into a cradle so that if she jerked suddenly and slipped, she wouldn't get hurt, even though she wasn't doing much jerking. I wanted Aurora to see that she could trust me, that I was solid. As she pulled Ashley from my arms and put her back in the baby seat, her towel came undone and droplets from her wet hair sprinkled into the baby's face. It was eight in the morning and Aurora already looked tired. There were dark circles under her eyes that make up didn't cover anymore.

That Fourth of July, we went to Atlanta to be with Aurora's family. The holiday seemed even bigger there than it was in New York. Music piped through speakers at gas stations, firecrackers popped randomly throughout the day, and there was an American flag hanging from every door and storefront and car window. Everybody was anxious to see the new baby and it was a parade as soon as we walked through the door. They had balloons and streamers and tables loaded with cupcakes covered in pink icing and white bonnets made of sugar. Aurora was relaxed and it felt like we had passed through a television screen and into a sitcom world where everyone was beautiful and funny, and where any conflicts were resolved within a half an hour, all with a sweet southern drawl.

Hot dogs and hamburgers and sausage links were continuously sizzling on the barbecue. There was potato salad, string beans, homemade coleslaw and corn bread stacked everywhere. They had Randy Travis on the record player alternating with Ray Charles and Motown classics. I ate pigs feet for the first time, and though I didn't really like them, there was nothing that I would have refused from that place. There were apple trees in the back and I could run barefoot outside and feel my feet sink into soft soil under the grass. It wasn't the house Aurora and her sisters had grown up in, but I pictured her running across the open field down by the pool playing tag with them, eating popsicles with their feet dangling lazily in the water.

The first time Aurora hit me was on the first day back to school. That morning was particularly rough on her and it was more than the heavy blink of her eyelids, or the jittery way she wrung her hands and pulled on her sleeves. Every now and then her eyes would fill with tears and she'd put Ashley down to rush to the bathroom. She'd come back smelling like cigarettes and air freshener with an empty look on her face. Her pregnancy cravings seemed to have never passed and she continued to have random dessert foods for breakfast, or packaged snacks throughout the day. The difference was that now she didn't want to be seen eating them. If I walked in the room after she'd just stuffed a piece of cold sausage in her mouth, she slammed her palm on the closest surface in anger and I turned right back around.

I had been her helper with the baby all summer. She never asked me to come to the rocking seat or the playpen to entertain the baby, but I knew when she needed a hand and when I appeared, she breathed easier. Usually I danced around to distract Ashley and she'd giggle instead of wail. Sometimes I blew a quick breath into her face and it startled her into a moment of silence that I used to give her a pacifier. I would lure her eyes with mine and stick out my tongue or make crazy faces until she was transfixed.

That morning I stood in front of my bedroom mirror getting ready for school, contemplating what shoes to wear. I thought maybe my leather sandals since we were having an Indian summer. They had two straps going across and one long strap down the middle with a gold buckle on the side. I finally decided it was better to wear the closed penny loafers with ankle socks since it was my first day, and it was a Catholic school after all. I came down the stairs with butterflies in my stomach about meeting all new kids and teachers.

"Rorie, what do think about these shoes for my first day?"

When I turned the corner at the landing I saw her fussing with the ironing board. She kicked it into the corner when it finally folded closed. The baby was wiggling in her car seat already, threatening to start screaming. Aurora's stockings had a long run on the left leg and she still had curlers dangling in her hair. My father had already left for the office and she was supposed to drive me to school for the first day. The clothes she'd worn before she was pregnant didn't quite fit yet, but she tried to make them work. Her blue blazer didn't button and the waist on her peach skirt couldn't fasten so she put on a wide blue belt that dug into her belly but hid the zipper. She dressed Ashley in a peach jumper to match her skirt, but when she put on the grey bundler it messed up the mommy/baby coordination. She considered letting Ashley go without the bundler, but it was still September no matter what the weatherman said.

She was yanking the last rollers out of her hair when she turned to me with a look I did not recognize and I froze right where I stood. It wasn't the harried scowl or the weary droop of the past several weeks. It was something else.

"Are these all right?" I asked.

She didn't answer. I searched, through the compartments of my mind, but there was no explanation for the sick feeling rising, spreading, swelling from my gut. I wanted to run to her, press my face against her bosom and breathe in her perfume to swallow the feeling back down. The seconds pounded past with a wrecking ball sound and the look in her eyes paralyzed me. I should have looked away, I should have gone back upstairs, but it was too late. The next instant, my stomach lurched and I leaned forward as my scrambled eggs and sausage, lightly buttered toast and orange juice breakfast burst up and spilled out of my mouth.

I looked at the goopy mess in front of my shoes with a sting in the back of my throat. I waited for Aurora to call me "sugar", and tell me that everyone makes a mess sometimes, that it was going to be all right. I still believe that she became something else that day, not human anymore. Her eyes that were usually round and clear, pulled into red slits and her teeth gnashed on her trembling bottom lip. She gave some kind of hiss and dragged me by my shoulder into the kitchen. Her hands became claws squeezing around my throat. Words gritted out of her mouth, but I couldn't hear them. My arms fell slack at my sides and I closed my eyes, imagining that whatever this was would be over soon. The room went silent except for the sound of my heartbeat struggling through my neck and bulging at my temples. I didn't try to shake myself free and I didn't cry out. Just as the throbbing in my cheeks started fading to numbness, she let me go with a push. My legs wobbled under me and I leaned against the wall to keep from falling.

"Dammit! Now I gotta clean up this goddamned mess! Go on upstairs and wash up. We're running late as it is."

I didn't wait to be told twice. I stretched my hands out in front of me, staggering down the hall. I followed the pink carpet leading me up the stairs like aisle lights on an airplane. When I got to the bathroom I told myself that the water splashing on my face was washing away what had just happened. It had not happened. Rorie would never do anything to hurt me. She loved me.

I pressed the cold washcloth on my cheeks and kept telling myself I was fine and everything would be OK. With every other meeting of her knuckles to my bones over the next year, I became more and more OK.

❧

The old folks often compared something valuable to salt. I suppose it goes back to the days when salt was so precious it was even used as currency. They said it was magical and could even bring zombies back to life. The chemical composition had the power to reignite the spark that the *Bokor*'s poison had dulled in order to use them as slaves. Their eyes and ears could open again after a taste and they'd be able to run away to return to the lives they were plucked from. They say you should keep your salt in a safe place and use it sparingly, to make it last. They say that if you have salt out in the sun, you should watch for rain.

My father forgot all the things the old folks used to say. I don't recall him speaking to me in French or Kreyol at any time. Whenever I called him *Papi* instead of Dad he looked at me like I had food caught in my teeth. His accent, which was almost gone, was about the only Haitian thing about him left. He even mispronounced his own name to make it sound more American. *Sah-muell* became *Sam-yu-ull*, or oftentimes just Sam. He spent so much time at work that he ended up eating all sorts of packaged snacks and fast food on top of what Aurora prepared at home. After a doctor appointment where he was told to lose weight and to watch what he ate, he bought a bicycle and started circling Prospect Park a few times a week. A lot of times he would come home, change his clothes and go right back out to ride.

"Dad, do you have to go?"

"I'm just going in the park for a little while. What's the matter?"

"I don't want you to go."

"Why? You don't want me to be healthy?"

"Just stay home."

"Don't be a baby, Olive. Why don't you read one of your books, or something. I'll be back fast, you'll see."

I watched him awkwardly maneuver his bike through the vestibule doors. It was a fancy ten-speed with a tiny seat that disappeared when sat on it. He broke into a sweat just hoisting it up the three little steps to the ground entrance. He rode to the park and only went around two or three times, just enough to say he'd made the effort. Aurora always had something flaky or fluffy or crunchy as a reward when he came back that pretty much cancelled the cycling.

Some evenings when I waited for my father to return, it would start raining. It was the warm kind of shower that could clean cars and bend small tree branches. The drops were huge and when they smacked against the windows it sounded like a million knuckles knocking, begging to be let in. I thought about the rain coming down so hard that it would carry off the last bit of Haitian-ness my father had left. It would flood the park, our whole street, and he would return home, fully Americanized, to find that all his salt had been washed away. What would he do then?

❧

At school, I devoured any assigned reading in half the time the other students did and my book reports, emblazoned with A's, were posted on the back wall of the class. My teachers sent home glowing reports and praised me at parent-teacher night. But as well as I did at school, other things escaped me and caused problems at home.

In the mornings, I'd open my bedroom window, just a crack, to hear the sounds of birds chirping or of squirrels climbing through the ivy in the back yard. But I'd forget to close it before I came downstairs and we'd all leave the house for school and work. It was fall, so by the time Aurora came home from her errands, the whole top floor would be cold and it would take hours for the bedrooms to be comfortable again. Sometimes while I played with Ashley, the phone would ring and I'd go to answer it with her pacifier in my hand. I'd come back, having forgotten where I put the thing and it was my fault when Aurora couldn't make her stop crying. When things were my fault, I paid. My swollen cheeks and eyelids didn't hurt so much anymore, though. I learned to anticipate when her hand, that was still surprisingly soft, would crack against my face and only wince a little. If I was standing, and only took one step back after a slap, she'd thump her fist into my chest to make sure I stumbled three or four steps until my back hit against the wall. I kept my eyes down and waited until I could go drape a cold washcloth over my face to make the welts go down. I was the only one there with quiet eyes that seemed to capture all the things she didn't want anyone to know. I think she hurt me to make herself feel better, but I still loved her. That was my problem.

Halloween came around, and I didn't want to dress up. There were groups of kids with their parents strolling up and down our block with their plastic pumpkin buckets or decorated pillowcases. Aurora went all out with baskets of full size chocolate bars, individually wrapped gummy candies, suckers and gumballs. I stayed inside the vestibule gate and passed out handfuls of the sweets to the witches and superheroes that came to wail at our door while Aurora got Ashley dressed. It didn't matter that she was too young to have candy or even realize what Halloween was. She wanted to take her around a little bit because that's what everyone did. My father came home at a decent hour and Ashley was a puppy in a fuzzy one-piece suit with floppy ears and a tail. My father held her as Aurora adjusted her tiny mittens.

"Olive, you sure you don't wanna come along?" Aurora asked. "You can be a ghost. I bet I can make you a great ghost costume real quick. There's nothing to be scared of out there."

Her voice drawled like honey over cinnamon rolls as she said my name. She wore diamond stud earrings and her hair was set in those perfect soft curls. The orange scarf draped elegantly around her neck made her look bright and festive, like a caramel Halloween cupcake. But her eyes were not the same. There was a bite there that gave me goose bumps and took away my voice.

"I'm not scared of what's out there," I said.
I glanced at my father trying to send him a telepathic code to tell him what I was really afraid of. But he didn't hear me.

❧

I started losing weight at an alarming rate. I was able to have my lunch at school or when my father took me to see Grandma Hélène on weekends, but my appetite vanished when it came time to eat at home. Nothing Aurora made tempted me anymore. I think she was bothered by my refusals and started going to all sorts of lengths to prepare my favorite things: fried chicken, lasagna, spaghetti and meatballs. She ordered General Tsao's chicken from the fancy Chinese place in Park Slope and we picked up Big Bacon Classic meals from the Wendy's next to the car wash after grocery shopping, but nothing really worked. I had a few bites that I chewed endlessly, but could never finish my meal. I passed over my beloved Cheese Doodles and Snickers bars, and left pepperoni pizza untouched.

At my twelfth birthday party, Aurora ordered a gigantic five-foot Blimpie sandwich that was cut into 25 slices to serve to my friends. I thought there was way too much meat and the shredded lettuce kept falling out and made a mess everywhere, but everyone there thought it was great. She layered four giant homemade chocolate chip cookies into a cake. There was custard and berries in between the layers and the whole thing was iced with pink frosting with my name spelled out in tiny chocolate chips beneath a number twelve candle. Everyone gathered around me in the dining room to sing happy birthday and clapped as I blew out the flame.

"This is so cool! Olive, your mom is the best!" some kid I didn't even know gushed as she skipped off with the slice I handed her.

I looked over at Aurora scooping up Ashley and smiling with the milling parents holding paper plates of cookie cake and plastic cups of soda. Tears crept up and I slipped away to the bathroom to hide them. When my eyes were dry again, I dumped my piece of cake and went back to the party.

❧❧

As I got skinnier, my father got fatter. His doctors gave him pills and advice on diets and fitness routines, but his collars only got tighter and the hair on the back of his head was perpetually slicked down from perspiration. He started taking me to all sorts of specialists for consultations and testing. The pediatrician tapped my knees with a little rubber hammer and looked into my ears. He pressed a cold stethoscope against my chest and my back and told me to take deep breaths. He checked my blood and my urine and when the results came back, he confirmed that I wasn't sick. I don't know how he was able to tell. He put a lead blanket over my body and pushed me through a laser dome. He told me to stay completely still so a machine could look into my brain. The loud buzzing and clanging drowned out my feeling of being a science experiment and actually lulled me to sleep. I traveled to another dimension, leaving my thin body behind. I floated through the walls and out of the hospital without anyone noticing. I flew over trees, over buildings, over entire neighborhoods and highways until I got to the ocean. The water was calm and reached out to infinity. But soon my invisible wings gave out. I was exhausted and started falling in slow motion. I wanted to call out, but I knew that no one would hear my voice. I knew that there would be no one to save me before I hit the water and drowned. The lights came back on and the nurse came to help me up. I slouched up to my elbows on the examination table in a cotton gown with balloons printed all over it. My tongue felt heavy and dry. I looked down at my bony arms.

"Sir, she's as healthy as a horse. I can't see anything wrong with her," the doctor said.

One weekend when my father was actually home, I sat in the living room with my face behind a book listening to the muffled rise and fall of voices as he and Aurora talked upstairs. I could never make out what they were saying when they argued, but I always thought it was about me. Straining to listen, I stayed on the same page going over the same few lines of my book over and over. It was Edgar Allen Poe and I loved his sad creepy tone. There was a familiar darkness to all his stories, and almost no happy endings. The one I liked the most was The Pit and the Pedulum. I put myself in that medieval cell, crawling and feeling in the dark for anything recognizable. I knew that it was me strapped down to a plank with a blade counting the inevitable downward strokes until the moment of my death. In my final breaths before falling down the yawn of disaster, there was hope that a switch would flip, that some hand would crack through the wall and save me. I breathed through that anxiety every time I turned those pages, holding on to the hope of the same kind of miracle.

The stairs creaked under my father's weight as he came down. I had to use the bathroom but didn't want to run into him in the narrow hallway, so I waited. When I heard him reach the landing I got up slowly. I walked along the wall, careful not to take up too much space. I rubbed my face against the rose striped wallpaper as I stepped silently down the hall and tried to become part of the woodwork.

"Hi Dad."

My father lingered where he stood as I crept closer. His belly and the roll under his chin seemed bigger than ever as he pulled out a handkerchief to wipe the back of his neck. The cotton polo top he had on was from the Big & Tall department, but the short sleeves still squeezed around his shoulders and biceps and made him look uncomfortable. He reached out to me with awkward affection. I went to him and we stood in front of the mirror in the foyer looking at ourselves. He folded his heavy arms around my shoulders.

"Are you all right?"

I looked into his eyes in the mirror and nodded, thinking the words I wouldn't say. *Why did you bring me here? She's killing me.* I prayed hard for magic to fill the room like a ball of light. I prayed that he would open his eyes and realize what was going on and save me.

"Yeah, Dad. I'm fine."

It turns out, he was the one that needed saving. The long hours he kept at work, the fake exercise he put in, the rich salty foods he ate, the snacking even when he wasn't hungry; all these things contributed to his health withering upon itself like rose petals curling in fresh flames. One week later, my father collapsed at his office and died of a massive stroke.

Aurora's family came up for the funeral and filled the house with noise and activity that made it feel like we were back in Atlanta again. Her sisters stayed with us while their husbands and children went to hotels. Aurora hardly spoke or ate or had any expression. I couldn't tell whether she was heartbroken or angry and struck dumb and in need of a Haitian remedy that would bring her dead eyes back to life again. I wanted to go to her. There was a window where we could be close again and cling to each other for comfort, but her sisters kept a steady hover and I couldn't find a single moment that I could make ours. They washed her hair, did the laundry and the dishes. They cooked and straightened and swept and took care of Ashley who was a year and a half and very fussy. At the church, Aurora handed her to her oldest sister who carried her to the church entrance while people filed down the aisle to lay flowers in the open casket. People I had never met before touched my face and looked at me with pity. When it was my turn to place a flower on my father's chest, I couldn't do it. Instead I tried one last time to send him a message with my thoughts. This time I know he heard me. The invisible wall between us was gone, but it was too late. I crushed my flower in my palm. There was no time for tears. I was alone with Aurora.

❧❦

In the days after everyone was gone, I stepped even more quietly than before. I lined my books and tapes in alphabetical order on the desk in my room, and arranged my shoes neatly on the floor of my closet. I smoothed and straightened the comforter on my bed and placed my stuffed animals by size on the pillow. Then I stood in front of my mirror and slapped myself. I stared into my eyes and hit both cheeks one at a time. I did it slowly at first, then harder and faster until my skin started to sting and swell. When I lost my breath and felt the burning heat in both my face and my palms, I stopped. I went in the bathroom and pressed a cold washcloth against my cheeks to soothe the welts and forced my lips into a smile.

After about a week of this pre-emptive practice, I was able to swallow any tears before they crept up until they stopped coming altogether. At school, I followed my classmates to their games, even though I didn't jump or run or do anything that caused me to break a sweat or mess up my hair. They shrugged and pulled me along because I was agreeable, but I'm sure they all thought I was weird.

One morning when spring was once again pushing early into summer, the breeze that danced between the leaves outside didn't make it through the open classroom windows. Ms. Galdorisi paced through the rows of desks fanning herself with a piece of green oak tag paper. She opened the classroom door to create some airflow, but it was no use. When I started to feel perspiration moisten my palms and forehead, I took off my cardigan and hung it on the back of my chair. Five seconds later the girl sitting behind me whispered, "Oooh, look at your shirt…"

On the back of both of my white sleeves there were four equally spaced maroon slits that looked like bite marks from a shark who gave up too easily. When I pulled at the fabric to get a better look, it peeled from my skin like it had been glued there. I remembered how my blouse had gotten that way, and I quickly put my cardigan back on.

I was at the kitchen table that morning staring at my bowl of oatmeal. It was the instant kind that you poured hot water over to mix into a paste of cinnamon raisin or baked apple or maple sugar. I turned my spoon around and around in the warm beige mush, but I couldn't eat it. I tried to come up with a reason to go back upstairs; a forgotten earring, or a book, but I couldn't think of a lie fast enough and just squirmed with anxiety. Aurora leaned over me, adjusting her hot rollers.

"What are you doing?" she asked.

"Nothing," I said, bracing. "I'm eating."

"No you're not. You're sitting there trying to make yourself throw up, aren't you?"

"No."

She yanked me out of my seat and stood me up in front of her. Both hands wrapped around my thin upper arms and her nails dug in.

"What the fuck am I supposed to do with you? Every day you pull this shit on me, every goddamn day!"

She shook me until my neck started snapping back and forth and I accidentally bit my tongue.

"Say something, dammit!"

Of course I couldn't. She let me go and I clung to the back of the chair with my eyes on the floor, which was swaying like waves. I knew not to look an adult in the eye when I was being scolded, but she stood there glaring at me with her hands clawed just waiting for me to make a sound. I was close enough to smell her perfume, and the heat of her anger made the scent of Trésor spread around me like arms. I had loved that scent, I breathed it in back when she used to hug me and caress my face and murmur motherly sweetness to me even though I wasn't her child. I wanted to be forgiven for whatever I did to ruin us, for letting my father die. I was willing to take the blame for anything, even that, as long as it made her happy with me again. I closed my eyes and felt my arms reaching up to the Trésor, but she snapped me back to reality.

"Wake up, you idiot, I'm talking to you!"

Her palm whacked the side of my face. Hot breath blew from her nose like a dragon and my stomach turned. I felt the urge to vomit, but I hadn't even taken one spoonful of my oatmeal so my stomach had nothing to give. My stifled heaving made her even angrier and she dragged me to the backyard door to shove me into the little powder room where she smoked her cigarettes.

When I was finished lurching yellow bile, I rinsed my mouth and felt the throbbing on the backs of my arms, but I ignored the pain. I willed it away, until the girl in class reminded me that it was still there.

By then I was a zombie plodding through days without emotion. Even when I was being choked and slapped and called "lethargic" at home, my tears wouldn't fall. Even when Aurora moaned about how much I looked like my father or about my mother not giving a damn about me, my face remained stone. Only at night did I allow any sadness to surface. I was a kid and I could still be scared and long for miracles. But there was no room for miracles in that house, so one day I tried to stop.

It was just before dusk on a Sunday, and I was coming back from the butcher on Flatbush Avenue. As I turned down Midwood, I wished that the walk home were longer. Some kids were throwing a ball back and forth and others were hanging out on a crumbly brownstone stoop licking artificial cheese powder off their fingertips. With a heavy paper bag full of meat in my arms I walked by a heated game of Red Light, Green Light going on in the middle of the street and for a moment I longed to be part of it. These kids were dirty and sweaty and loud. They had ashy legs and untied sneakers. Their hair was unruly and they sucked their teeth loudly when a car interrupted their game. They looked so comfortable, as though playing in the middle of the street, dodging cars and teasing pedestrians was the most fun they could have in the whole world.

At the corner of Midwood and Bedford, those sounds of fun faded away and my heartbeat filled my ears. What would happen if I just disappeared? If something really bad happened in the next few seconds, would the pain flare and then burn away? Something like a mugger slicing my throat, or maybe a car slamming into my skinny body? A steady thumping was coming closer and my feet floated off the ground one in front of the other. *"...we're gonna have happy times together..."* The roaring of a souped-up engine was gaining and there was a long honk with voices yelling for me to get out of the way, but I kept floating, bracing my arms around the bag of meat. When the roar seemed to surround me, a terrible screech sliced the air and suddenly the music moved through my body like a bolt of ice. It didn't matter that the driver didn't stop to make sure I was okay. It made no difference that he cursed while violently spinning his steering wheel to avoid me. He had the green light, there was no accident, and he was gone. My next step landed hard on the firm asphalt and I melted into burning tears of defeat.

ॐ

When my sixth grade class attended church services during the school year, we were taught to dip our fingers in the marble fountain of holy water at the entrance and cross ourselves as we filed solemnly into pews and kept our heads bowed. A man in a stiff robe droned on, arranging a shiny gold chalice and a platter of tasteless wafers on the altar. When it was my turn I touched the blessed drops to my forehead, chest, and shoulders, convinced I was creating a force field that would keep a life-saving reserve of air in my lungs for when Aurora was choking it out.

I lost myself in the echoes and whispering shadows that seemed to live only in church. I learned to appreciate silent contemplation and the hypnotic quality of hymns being sung in a space with high vaulted ceilings and stained glass windows. I closed my eyes and told myself that I believed. I slowed my mind and my heartbeat. I wrapped myself in a cloak that protected me from Aurora's too bright light. I didn't want to fear her, I wanted to belong to her. I wanted her to feed me one of her tasty dishes and turn me into another girl with no past and no memory. No former life, no crazy mother, no smelly clothes in cramped closets; only fresh t-shirts and jeans, clean sheets, neat hair, and a house full of pink carpet and glossy old wood.

From the depths of my blankets, I cried out to the Lord that so many people talked about, and knelt to, and wept to. I closed my eyes at night and sent my prayers silently up over me, past my swollen eyes and sore ribs and heart-busting panic. My fingers folded and squeezed together and became slippery as I rocked back and forth in private passion. I cultivated faith that went beyond the catechism taught in class. The other kids yawned or passed notes while the teacher told us about Daniel in the lion's den, but I was captivated by that story. Aurora was King Darius and I forgave the weakness that made her condemn me. I looked past her confusion and I believed that God would not let me be eaten by beasts. I shushed my classmates, but they just rolled their eyes and exchanged Jolly Ranchers while the teacher told us about Jochebed sending her baby down the river in a basket to keep him from being killed. I listened and prayed, and tried to imagine how I would be saved.

I woke up in the middle of the night to the sound of crying. At first I thought I was dreaming but the closer I listened I realized it wasn't Ashley's fire engine wail, but something deeper and softer. I slipped out of bed and crept into the hall. I found that the sobs and half formed words were coming from Aurora's room. A rush of cold stopped me in my tracks, but I couldn't turn back. My nightgown felt two sizes too big and it dragged on the floor behind me. My toes sank into the carpet, stepping over the familiar creaks until I reached her open door. She was curled into a ball under her sheets. She looked like a child who was lost in the cold, hiding from a monster, praying for rescue. I couldn't understand her mumblings, but I knew the ache in her voice. Her whimpering was soaked in loneliness and fear. I crept closer and climbed into bed with her. I wrapped my arms around her waist and pressed my cheek against her back.

"Don't cry, Rorie. We'll be all right. I love you..."

My tears were still frozen in my center, but as I held Aurora close, trying to soothe her, calling on the healing powers I used to have, I felt them melting and rushing back in a wave. Her body quieted for a moment and she turned. I touched her face, my small hand was cold against her flushed cheek and she pressed it closer. We were head to head and I closed my eyes. I silently recited the Hail Mary, thankful for this tenderness. When I reached *the hour of our death*, the back of my head slammed into the nightstand.

I slid to the floor, and when I opened my eyes Aurora was screaming and crying and ripping the sheets and pillows from the bed. She stomped around the room, yanking open dresser drawers and flinging clothes everywhere. I tried to crawl out of the room on my hands and knees but she knocked over the television set and it landed on my leg. Aurora stood over me trembling like a building that had been rigged with explosives and was finally collapsing. The stone façade crumbled and sent chips into my eyes. The bricks burst loose from the decayed mortar and fell, smashing onto my shoulders and the top of my head. Heavy panes of glass exploded from their frames and rained down shards that cut my arms and legs as I tried to roll away. I heard Ashley crying, I heard Aurora screaming over sirens wailing. I heard my heartbeat slowing down, down, down. Until there was nothing.

❧

The first thing I remember was the smell of boiled chicken and industrial floor cleanser when I finally woke up. The squeaking of little metal wheels passing by trailed in the distance. I was aware of layers of thin fabric on my skin and of being afraid to move. I swallowed and felt a general heaviness on my face. I drew a breath deeply through my nose and pushed it out slowly.

"*Ollie, chérie?* Are you awake now?"

I recognized my grandmother Hélène's voice. It had been a few months since I'd seen her. Before my father died, he used to drop me off at her apartment on Sundays so she and I could spend the day watching sitcoms or nature shows and speak French during commercials. She was my only link to my mother and I suppose he saw it as his duty to preserve that. Grandma Hélène was never much of a cook and she made the only dish that she truly mastered every time I came. Bread soup was not an ideal meal for someone who vomited all the time, but I always finished my bowl with no problems. She'd tell me that it was good for the blood and that it would protect me from catching cold. During our visits, she'd absently squeeze my arm and shoulder while we learned about the life cycle of frogs in South America or laughed at Jack Tripper and his shenanigans with Janet and Chrissy.

"Nurse, excuse me, nurse? My granddaughter is waking up. Please…"

Grandma held her tiny clutch under her arm and waved a gloved hand in the doorway. The sound of thick thighs cased in cotton brushing against each other approached and stopped at my bed. A warm heavy body pressed against the metal safety railing and leaned over me.

"You awake, little lady? Can you look at me?"

I raised my eyebrows to help my lids open and saw my grandmother sitting in a chair near the foot of my bed. She took off her gloves and rubbed my left leg. I wanted to ask what happened, why I was there, but the look on her fragile face told me that the mere sound of my voice would melt it into a mess of concealer and blush. I blocked the thought from my mind and blinked slowly. I rolled my eyes over to the nurse and watched as she adjusted the fluid bag hanging next to me and checked the IV flow to my arm. She called me honey and sweetheart, but didn't smile. None of the nurses could bring themselves to look into my face for longer than the moment it took to ask how I was feeling, or if I needed to be cleaned up. I only shook or nodded my head slightly and gave slow blinks.

There were two other people sharing the room with me but I never saw them since the curtain around my bed was always pulled. I was hardly able to move because of the brace around my left knee, and the one around my neck cushioning my face. There were bandages on my elbows and forearms protecting cuts and gashes. The stitch job on my forehead was smeared with ointment and left uncovered. A couple of my ribs were fractured and the side of my top lip was swollen. My grandmother stood and spoke to the parade of nurses and doctors who filed at my bedside, gently touching, examining, shining pen-lights into my eyes, and checking the dressings on my wounds. Some of them stayed at the foot of my bed holding clipboards. Their foreheads furrowed as they looked me over, taking notes. They nodded awkwardly and shuffled out of the room when the attending physician finished speaking to my grandmother.

From the first day I was brought in, I was sedated for the pain and didn't speak. What was there to say? What did I remember? Did I know where I was? Did I know how I got there? My eyes rolled toward the bare window near my bed. I couldn't see anything but the sky and the tops of a few trees, but I was grateful for that bit of nothingness. I wasn't ready to feel afraid or to wonder about Aurora and Ashley. I couldn't think about those things yet, if I did I'd go crazy. I decided to wait another day for those thoughts to fill my head and focused only on the pain that throbbed in all my joints, in my ribs if I breathed too deeply, and on all my patches of injured skin. The medication they gave me periodically cooled the excruciating flares, but kept me in a lull. I didn't speak to anyone, not even to my grandmother, but every day, when the sun's reddest rays tangled in those bare branches outside the window, I pushed a whisper through my dry mouth and prayed: *Hail Mary full of grace, the lord is with thee. Blessed art thou among women...*

I had been in the hospital for thirteen days floating in and out of medicated stupor, and I still wasn't ready to be scared. I was able to stretch out my right leg to stand on my own, and shuffle to the bathroom with a crutch, but I needed help once I got there. My lip was back to normal size and I was chewing my food. I was able to ask for what I wanted and tell the nurse where the pain throbbed the most. Grandma Hélène came to see me every day in a dress and short gloves. I turned my lips up just enough to give her a little smile and watched her folded fingers squeeze together in thanks.

One late afternoon the curtain was pulled back and my bed was adjusted so I could better see the television, but I kept my eyes on the window. I could see more trees, the parking lot, and a piece of the highway. A nurse came in to change my pain medication. About twenty minutes after she squeezed it into the line that already fed into my arm, my eyelids became heavy and I felt like I was swimming in warm water. The sun was starting to set and I recited my prayer barely moving my lips. *Holy Mary, mother of God, pray for us sinners...*

Grandma Hélène had stepped away to get some more watery coffee from the machine down the hall. She usually stayed with me until visiting hours were over or until I fell asleep. I fought the heaviness draping my eyes until she came back but my blinks lasted longer and longer. I was slipping off when I felt a heavier blanket pull gently onto my legs. I opened my eyes but didn't turn my head. The sun was almost gone, only a thin red line was left pushing up from the earth fading up to pale orange, translucent yellow, reaching up to the beginnings of deep blue. A hard hand cradled my feet, moved over my knees, rested on my hip, touched my shoulder, gathered my hand into its own and held it.

In that moment, I knew it was time to feel. I became afraid. My skin erupted in goose bumps that actually hurt as they crawled over my arm. When I trembled, the hand squeezed mine. My heart pumped faster and faster until I could feel it in my throat and I started to sweat. The hand reached up and touched the tears that were finally running down the side of my nose. My chest started heaving as all the thoughts I had put on hold came rushing to the front of my brain to be claimed. My mother was lost. My father was dead. My stepmother would probably be carted off to jail or a mental hospital for trying to kill me. My little sister would be shuffled around in the care of family members and would grow up to hear horrible stories about both her parents. And this was all because of me. The hand cupped my chin and turned my face. I shut my eyes, ready to trust the next person I saw when I opened them. And there she was. Mary Moses had heard my prayers and had come to save me. I was rambling, incoherently though sobs, about Aurora and Ashley, my father, Carly, everything that wouldn't fit in my skinny chest anymore.

It's all right now. You're safe.

In the middle of weeping, I gave in to the drip
moving though my veins, drawing me into soft
waves of sleep. I closed my eyes and I don't know
how much time passed before my body was lifted
out   of   the   water.

5 Mary Moses

On Christmas Eve, I peeled up our block in a rented silver BMW. The heated seats vibrated from the bass and though the windows were rolled up, the nasal wail of Beny Moré's *"Maracaibo"* seeped through the glass and bounced against the icicle-covered houses outside. The street was empty, but I'm sure there was at least one face peeking from behind a curtain to see what the racket was on the night of the savior's birth. I pulled up to our house and burst out of the car, stumbling into the snow that was banked up to my waist along the driveway. I laughed without feeling the chunks that stuck to my stockings and clumped onto my snakeskin heels. I was sweating so I left my coat in the passenger seat and went to the trunk for the gift-wrapped box I'd brought. I spent almost a whole minute struggling with my key and almost stumbled in the door when it finally gave.

"Hey! Hi! Hi, everybody! *Joyeux Noël!*" I kicked off my shoes on the doormat before continuing in. Everybody was in the living room with the fireplace going and Nat King Cole filling the place with classic roasted chestnuts. Uncle Aaron and Peter were slapping down dominoes and Jude was pouring his chunky blonde girlfriend a drink. They all dropped their mouths open at the sight of me, but before anybody had a chance to say anything I set my gift-wrapped box down by the staircase and rushed to kiss each person on both cheeks. Even though I called sometimes and sent packages to the house, it had been almost two years since I'd been home.

"Uncle! *Petee! Judee!* Oh, hello, I'm Olive, their sister. Well, we're really cousins, but I'm *basically* their sister!" I couldn't stop giggling and Jude's poor girlfriend giggled with me, not sure whether I was making fun of her or not.

"Oh hi, Jude told me so much about you. I didn't recognize you from the pictures!"

I scanned the photos around the room and found softer, fuller versions of my face smiling with a basketball, someone's hand giving me rabbit ears, a dumb hairstyle with frizzy bangs. I wiped my forehead with my silk sleeve.

"Oh, look at this! You guys got a live tree? I can't believe it, since when? So nice!"
Mary Moses came out of the kitchen and I almost tripped on the edge of the rug rushing over to her.

"*Mamou!* Mamou, how are you? Merry Christmas! Oh, my God, I love your hair, the little afro looks so good on you. OK, I have something for you... But we should wait until midnight when we do the exchange, right? Yeah, that's better. Mamou, I'm starving! What do we have?"

I kissed my aunt on both cheeks and left her standing by the kitchen doorway with her mouth in a tight line. I picked over the platters arranged on the coffee table like I hadn't had a meal in days. I stuffed my mouth with mini fish patties, chunks of broiled pork sprinkled with *pikliz*, cheese and grapes, all while telling some stupid story about the traffic on the Jacques-Cartier bridge that probably made no sense to anyone anyway. They all chuckled at my clowning, except for Mary Moses who only sipped tea and watched my hands and my eyes.

"Hmm, you did lime juice instead of vinegar. So good. Hmm, did you add something else to your *pikliz*? You're always adding something…" She didn't answer, so I just kept going.

"So this guy from *La Revue Gastronomique* comes in like three months ago and thinks he's all incognito with a silk scarf around his neck and huge glasses tryna look like Andy Warhol or something…"

"Oh God, here we go!"

Peter and Jude were used to my stories by now. At first, they didn't believe the crazy things that supposedly always happened at the restaurant. They thought I made it all up for laughs, until I insisted that they drop in randomly to check things out for themselves.

"You're not gonna make me believe that a restaurant like Maison Boussougou would actually let a dog eat at the table, Olive! Come on!"

"Listen, you don't know who that dog knows!"

"Oh, please! That's just crazy, those rich downtown people would never go for that shit. And what about tourists? Health codes?"

"What about them? Dude, you'd be surprised what people will go for if you put it in a really nice plate."

The first time Jude came to the restaurant, I wasn't even there. When he asked the waitress about me, apparently she insisted that she didn't know anyone by that name. He assumed the girl was new or something because I had been at that restaurant for five years and I had made the reservation for him in advance. During the course of his meal, which was completely divine, he asked every other server about me and they all answered the same way: Who? No, I'm sorry, I don't know who that is. By the time his dessert came, the chef brought it to him personally. But instead of it being the *crème brûlée* he ordered, it was a ramekin of black olives neatly covered in whipped cream and sprinkled with brown sugar. He got on me for that one for months.

At midnight we opened presents. The new girlfriend gave Mary Moses and Uncle Aaron a candle set that smelled like lavender. The boys gave each other baseball caps and fancy pens, and gave their parents matching robe and slipper sets. I made a big deal about saving my present for last and watched impatiently as Mary Moses peeled off the wrapping paper to reveal an expensive, state-of-the-art juicer with all sorts of attachments and recipe leaflets. I had jabbered all night about the health benefits of carrot juice, beet juice, apple juice, and ginger juice. I went on about how it was giving me so much energy and was better than coffee. I went to open a window while Uncle Aaron and the guys exchanged uncomfortable smiles and praised the gift. Jude's girlfriend, whose name I was told but didn't remember, nodded along with everyone else, but I was looking for my aunt's reaction. Even with the music playing in the background (uncle Aaron loved his American holiday standards), the silence pressed in and made my heart pound in my ears. I picked at a hangnail on my thumb and waited, but she just stared at me like I was a brown speck on a white dress that no one wanted to mention.

The empty air was drawing too much attention to me so I continued to fill it with more prattle about another food critic who came into the restaurant and actually stood up and sang the Haitian national anthem after he finished his meal, then gave the restaurant an amazing review, and about a celebrity baby shower barbeque I had catered, and a birthday brunch I was planning for Uncle Aaron in the spring. I was moving too fast to give anyone a chance to question me about anything. But I could tell that from her seat at the table Mary Moses was following my pace, seeing the thing that I was trying to hide.

"You're not fooling anyone here, Olive. How long do you think you can keep fooling yourself?" Her even voice cut through every other sound like a machete.

"Huh?"

"You think anybody in this house needs these fancy things you keep buying?"

"Mamou, it's Christmas." My smile was cajoling, or at least it was trying to be.

"I know what day it is. Do *you* know what day it is? Do you know what planet you're on?"

"What?" I chuckled and reached for a napkin to wipe my nose.

"Marie Lourdes, please. *Cherie,* this is not the time..." Uncle Aaron tried to reach across the table for her arm, but she pulled it away. She continued without taking her eyes off me.

"Oh no? Then when? When she's lying in a gutter somewhere? When we get a call from the hospital telling us that they did everything that they could do? Or better yet, when the police come to our door asking questions we wish we didn't know the answers to?"

The guys looked at each other with wide eyes. Uncle Aaron squinted and blinked like someone had blown smoke in his face. The chunky girlfriend was stranded on her chair with a glass of white wine warming in her hand. I stood up, smoothing my hair, sweating even more.

"Mamou, I don't know what you're talking about. Lying in a gutter? What does that even mean?"

"Don't play stupid, my girl. Don't you dare do that to me!"

Now Mary Moses was on her feet. The full height of her was intimidating and I was suddenly afraid. Her small eyes covered every inch of me and I felt exposed. Proof or no proof, I knew she could see what I had done and there was no way I could run from my punishment. I think maybe I wanted to be found out. Maybe I'd been leaving a trail of crumbs to myself all along. Leaving clues for them. For you. But in that moment, almost before midnight, her steady voice that had always calmed my nerves, made me tremble. The pits of my blouse were soaked through and my cheeks kept quivering.

"Marie Lourdes, Olive is an adult ..." Uncle Aaron tried to diffuse the crackle that was building in his wife's voice, but she couldn't hear him.

"You think I don't know what I'm seeing, Olive? You think I don't know what I know?"

"What do you want me to say, Mamou?"

I was rubbing my eyes, inching up and down on my toes, tapping my thigh. I used my sleeve to wipe my forehead and cheeks, regretting raising my voice to her, but it was too late to slow down.

"I always work. I don't live off any man. I drive a nice car that I pay for and I live in a nice place. I have earned the right to hurt somebody!"

"Oh? And you choose to hurt the people who love you? The people who have done everything for you?"

"That's not what I meant, Mamou, please..."
I was breathing hard, dizzy, waiting for her to crush me with whatever she would say next. A pop from the fireplace made me jump and I wanted to scream. Nothing coming out of my mouth was making any sense and I knew it, but I had lost control. When Mary Moses spoke again there was no firepower in her voice. She had put down her weapons and surrendered.

"I see that I spent all these years washing my hands, only to wipe them on the floor," she said.
"I'm finished."

Nobody moved. Nobody spoke. Mary Moses gave me a long bitter stare then walked away from all of us. She went upstairs and we all listened to her footsteps going down the hall and the slamming of her bedroom door. We heard another slam and the sound of something breaking, but that anger was not for me. It was for a memory that wouldn't stay away no matter how many seeds she planted in the backyard, or how much cocaine I breathed up my nose. A draft crawled up my back and I remembered that I had left my coat in the car. I couldn't look at anyone in the face, but I knew they were all staring at me with pity or reproach, or something awful that I didn't want to see. I went to put on my shoes at the front door and found that my feet were swollen and wouldn't fit in them. I leaned against the wall, pushing and squeezing until I felt Uncle Aaron's hand on my shoulder.

"Olive... I don't know what to say, baby. Just, please take care of yourself. OK?" I nodded without turning around and hurried out the door.

❧

Marie Lourdes had always been an early riser. When she was a little girl in Haiti, her eyes always opened before the roosters crowed, before the sun rose above the hills. She would creep out of her room, stepping silently down the hall to the patio. She'd listen for her mother's movements in the bathroom and slide open the glass door. She leaned over the cement wall to look out at the rooftops of other large houses with patios. Their house was surrounded by the kind of trees children loved to climb and tear fruit from, but the children in this neighborhood didn't climb trees. Certainly not where their parents could see, and never in Colonel Edgar Séjour's yard. The mention of his name made teenage boys straighten their backs and made grown men lower their gaze. On the days he was home, even the dogs in the area barked less. But the morning moments that Marie Lourdes took were hers. Barefoot, she leaned over the cement wall and could almost reach a branch with a hanging mango. The wide leaves of a banana tree draped over the far side, and there was loose *kénèp* strewn on the floor near the table and chairs. When the roosters started calling, she came in and crept back to the room she shared with her sisters.

She was a proper eldest child. She completed her schoolwork neatly and made the best grades in her class. She recited her lessons without breaking rhythm or missing a word. She looked after her sisters in the schoolyard and was a silent partner to Mimose in hiding their shenanigans from Hélène's exasperated attempts at discipline. Whenever she broke a sweat wailing at the girls for dirtying their dresses or chewing like cows, she rushed in frustration into the bathroom. Marie Lourdes noticed that when her mother emerged she was calmer, with no more interest in yelling. She also wore a fresh layer of make-up that made her look even more damaged than before.

She knew that her sister Madeleine chewed her fingernails, sometimes down to the nub. One time, after a teacher had scolded her for bad penmanship, Madeleine bit her fingers until the raw flesh under the nail line bled and she couldn't write at all for days. They hid it from Hélène and Mimose dipped Madeleine's fingers in lemon juice and aloe to make her stop. Marie Lourdes always checked on her youngest sister, Mathilda, who slept a bit too peacefully. At times Marie Lourdes had to shake her and pinch her cheeks to pull her from a dream state that was disturbing.

She pulled her mother into the room one morning to show her how strange it was that it should take such effort to wake Mathilda. Hélène looked on as Marie Lourdes called into her sister's ear, tickled her feet, pulled off her sheets, shook her vigorously and even yanked her hair. Finally, Marie Lourdes got into bed with her sister and pulled her into a sitting position. She cradled her like a baby and hummed with her their cheeks pressed together until she opened her eyes. Upon waking, Mathilda was perfectly surprised to see her mother and sister hovering over her with their faces drawn with worry.

"Maman, this is not normal, is it? Why does she sleep so hard?"

Hélène picked at her nails and stared at her girls, from the oldest to the youngest. She had no answer, and that troubled her more than the question. Mathilda cuddled with her sister for a moment longer then bounced out of bed to head to the bathroom. Marie Lourdes waited for her mother to speak. Hélène bit at a piece of skin peeling from the cuticle of her thumb.

"Your sister is fine, Marie Lourdes. You know how she gets tired sometimes. You see? She is fine." Hélène hurried out of the room before her daughter could ask another question. Marie Lourdes sat for a moment looking at the empty space her mother left, then started making her sister's bed.

The girls enjoyed peeking at the cook while she prepared fresh meat for the next meal. They stood on chairs to look out the window to watch her squeeze lime juice into a bowl full of pork or goat. She rubbed it all vigorously with coarse salt before rinsing and making little slits in the flesh to let the spices and herbs seep through and marinate. This was as close as they would ever get to cooking in their younger years and they were never allowed anywhere near any slaughters. But in the first few weeks that she was there, Margo took Marie Lourdes to the far end of the yard and showed her how to kill a turkey.

She made the twelve year-old beanpole of a girl grab hold of the legs as she wrapped her fingers tight around the neck. The wide black wings flapped wildly and made Marie Lourdes lose her balance. She watched her grandmother draw a blade the length of her forearm from a fold in her skirt and slide the glint across the stretched neck of the bird. The first spurt of blood spattered Margo's skirt then flowed in a steady red line onto the dry dirt as she took the feet from Marie Lourdes and held the turkey upside down. There was to be no screaming, no crying, and certainly no turning away at the sight of blood. Margo instructed her stunned granddaughter to watch until the body gave its final twitch and went limp for good. Marie Lourdes kept blinking as the dead bird was lowered into the cauldron of boiling water. Her fingers found, with surprise, how easy it was to pull the feathers from the lifeless mass, leaving pale bumpy skin behind.

As Margo's visit stretched on, Marie Lourdes became her grandmother's shadow. She went with her on walks early in the morning to gather herbs for teas and balms, and to identify plants. The air was different so close to sunrise. The dew that veiled everything was like a trace of the bad dreams of the night before, but as the sun climbed higher, it burned it all away. Margo lit her pipe and waited just beyond the gate for her granddaughter to join her. They didn't speak as they walked out on the road beyond the property with canvas knapsacks and scissors. When they came home just as the cook was washing breakfast dishes, they set citrus peels out to dry and prepared jars of castor oil mixtures, or medicinal tea blends. It was in those days that Marie Lourdes started learning the way to part invisible seas and lead those who had been harmed to haven.

❧

Two weeks after checking me out of Kings County hospital, Mary Moses led me by the hand into her split-level brick house in Montréal. It was at the end of a long block and sat in a cul-de-sac with a small Flame Maple tree in the front yard. The house was quiet, except for classical music playing at low volume in the background. There was a pot of home stew simmering on the stove that scented the whole house. It was the kind that had big chunks of malanga, watercress, carrots, dumplings, and tender meat that dissolved between your teeth almost without chewing. The broth, seasoned with fresh garlic, scallions, thyme, parsley, salt, and cloves mashed together with a wooden mortar and pestle, was enough to cure almost any illness, and that aroma welcomed me better than any words could. I breathed it in and when I exhaled, a burden rolled off my chest. Uncle Aaron appeared at the kitchen door and I stepped weakly toward him. The space between us felt like a hundred slow motion miles and as I drew closer, I saw that the gentle smile on his face was hiding horror. Just two years earlier on summer vacation, I was a healthy kid who sang and played soccer with Jude and Peter in the park across the street. Now, the thing he pulled into in his arms had grayish teeth, a frightening skeletal body, and no songs. He held me close and I heard a muffled groan as I sank into his chest. I quickly pulled away and mustered a good practiced smile. I thought I was good at them, but there were tears sliding down my uncle's cheek as he took my face into his hands. "Darling, darling, I'm so happy to see you."

In the beginning, sleeping was a problem. I was in a place where the air no longer forced me to count my breaths, but I still feared that at any moment my new peace could be taken away. I constantly worried that someone would appear and decide that I was taking up too much space, or that I was already too much of a burden. I had lost both my parents and there was no place else for me to go. I routinely woke up in the middle of the night, disoriented. I went rigid under my covers, shoulders tight with panic and kept my eyes shut tight, waiting for the feeling to pass. I prayed, *Holy Mary, mother of God...*And she appeared. She tiptoed in the dark wearing a simple white nightgown and an old t-shirt covering her hair. She stopped at Peter's bed to adjust his sheets that were always hanging off him, kissed his face, and rubbed his pudgy belly. Then she came over to me and sat on my bed. I didn't move, but she knew I was waiting for her. She ran her hand over my thin back and felt how tense it was. She leaned in to touch my face and wiped away the tears she knew were there. She took my hand and held it until the tightness finally eased and let me drift off to sleep. Some nights she came in with a cup of tea with dried peels and leaves floating in it. Some nights she rubbed the back of my neck with oil that reminded me of church.

My body was frail and every day she applied her skills to the work of making it strong again. In those days, she was working as a registered nurse at Philippe Lemoyne hospital, but she had no intention of ordering prescriptions or shuttling me back and forth to appointments with specialists. After a battery of physical exams and blood tests confirmed that I was free of any medical conditions, she went to work on the rest. Every night at dinner, I was the last person to leave the table. She piled all our plates with fragrant rice and red beans, chicken braised with onions and garlic and herbs, simmered in tomato sauce. We all talked and laughed through dinner, but at first it was hard for me to get used to eating without the fear that it would immediately come back up again. My aunt ignored my worried frown and asked about my new teachers or what color Peter and I wanted our room to be painted. She paid no attention to my hesitation to go play outside with the neighborhood kids that I hadn't gotten to know yet. I mostly moped around the house in the beginning, but soon my desire to be with my cousins grew stronger than my fear of the happy kids and I finally joined them.

"How old are ya?
"What?"
"How old are ya?"

We were in the park and a boy from a few blocks over was asking me something, but I stood there looking at him like he was speaking Japanese or Martian. Jude jogged over with a deflated soccer ball he found in the bushes.

"Hey, how old is she?"

"Twelve. Olive, he wanted to know how old you are."

I tried to tilt my head to whisper to Jude that I didn't understand a word he said, but that was impossible since we were all practically within breathing space of each other.

"You don't speak French?"

I turned to look at Jude again feeling like I had just gone deaf. I watched my cousin be my interpreter in a language that all of us spoke, but for some reason I couldn't understand anything coming out of this kid's mouth. It turns out his Québec accent was much thicker than any I'd ever heard and he talked really fast on top of it. I couldn't stand the feeling of not fitting, so over time, a lot of time spent sitting in silence listening to my classmates, imitating inflections and memorizing slang, I was finally able to turn on that bushwhacking brogue and nobody could tell me I wasn't *pur laine*.

❧❧

"Come, you're going to help me today. Do you know how to cook?"

I looked up at my aunt and thought she was joking, but she didn't have a joking look on her face so I stifled the chuckle that came bubbling up my throat.

"Sandwiches. Eggs. Jello."

"Jello?"

"Yeah. You boil the water and mix in the powder, then you put it in the fridge to make it hard."

"You won't make that in this house. That's not food."

Mary Moses had a hard look and a stiff tone. Her skin was like brown velvet pulled tightly over her strong cheekbones and jaw, but she didn't scare me. I wanted to be near her, close enough to feel her warmth and smell her fragrance. She didn't wear perfume, but she did often smell like lavender or some other clean thing.

"Here. Take this."

She put a knife in my hand. There were small piles of scallions, bulbs of garlic, sprigs of thyme, cilantro, and parsley laid out on the counter. She balled her hand and lined her fingers up against a halved onion with her own knife and waited for me to do the same with mine. We sliced and chopped and diced our ingredients until there was a fragrant mound that we scooped with our hands and packed into a wooden *pilon*. She instructed me to sprinkle in pinches of salt and whole peppercorns and squeeze in a bit of lemon juice before she grasped the pestle and started to grind it all together.

Her grip was tight, but fluid. Her fingers opened and repositioned depending on the angle she needed to pound the flavors into harmony. The quick jabs created a thudding rhythm that hypnotized me into seeing sparks rise between her fingers and spill onto the counter. I thought they would singe the herbs and ignite the cotton curtains that hung over the window in front of us. I was afraid, but I couldn't wait to see how great a fire could come from Mary Moses' hands the more she pounded and mashed.

"*Tu vois?*" I nodded, rapt. She pointed the pestle under my nose so I could smell it.

The mixture rose into my nostrils and shot to my head like a flame. It rushed through my whole body with freshness and zest in a way that made time stop and go into warp speed at the same time. The whole kitchen was indeed on fire. There was no smoke and no sweat and amazingly nothing was destroyed, but the blaze spread and grew in frenzied circles all around the room and branded me from the inside out with smells and tastes that I knew would cling to me for the rest of my life. When I opened my eyes again, Mary Moses was smiling at my enchantment. She leaned over and kissed the top of my head.

"Look. I get some things in the market, but these herbs come from our garden in the yard. I'm putting you in charge of them, OK?

"Yes, Mamou. OK."

"You must water the soil and keep the rows neat. Everything we have is your ingredient. These are your tools."

At thirteen, I became used to having the smell of garlic or fresh herbs on my fingertips. After homework, or running around with my cousins, I always made my way to the kitchen to see if Mary Moses was in the middle of preparing something. If I had missed the prep, I tried to guess all the things that went into each dish.

"OK, what's in the *mayi moulin* tonight?"

"Cornmeal, dummy!" Peter moaned.

"Boy, when did we accept dummies into this house?" Mary Moses whacked him on the knuckles with the wooden spoon that was in the black bean sauce. We all laughed while he licked the back of his hand.

"Hmm, good mom!"

"There's something extra in it, right Mamou?"

She gave me a complicit wink that told me I was right, but I knew she wasn't going to just come out and tell me.

"I see the spinach, I know there's garlic, and salt of course, but there's another taste in here…"

"Why don't you just eat, little girl. It's getting cold."

I think I was a good apprentice. I made sure the aluminum pots and the cast iron skillets were scrubbed clean without being asked. I was careful not the let the wooden spoons soak too long in the dishwater so the tips wouldn't split. After homework and hanging out with friends, before going up to bed, I checked the windowsill and gathered any loose garlic skins and put them in the trash. On the weekends I made labels for the paper bags of dried things she kept in the pantry. There were herbs from our garden in the yard, peels, and roots and seeds that Mary Moses brought home double wrapped in fabric and tucked into a paper bag on the top shelf behind mason jars of salt and dried mushrooms. When Uncle Aaron's belly was swollen and hard, and his general doctor, the one whose word he trusted blindly, couldn't figure out what was wrong with him, Mary Moses mixed him a tea sprinkled with some of those strange ingredients and made him fast for three days. After a week, he was jogging around the park again and he started doing pushups in the backyard. The boys would go out to do them with him and they always ended up competing, leaving their father in a sweaty heap in the grass. Uncle Aaron never questioned Mary Moses' hands or her word. None of us did.

&

I know that for all the work that Mary Moses did to heal me, it was another soul that she was trying to yank back from the abyss. Every pound I gained was a victory. Every smile and burst of laughter I gave while playing Nintendo or copying dance moves from music videos was a triumph. She put her arms around me, but she was reaching through time for a memory. The memory would not be held, though. It wiggled and twisted like a tied goat trying to break free or a fish refusing to be reeled in. We both fought it through the years, and when I started hanging out later and later after school with my friends, it started to win. By the time I was in

CEGEP and coming home with bloodshot eyes, running up to my room explaining that I had to get started on a paper, the memory had taken the lead.

"Mamou, Uncle Aaron. I need to tell you something."

Jude was at football practice and Peter was off somewhere with his friends. Mary Moses and Uncle Aaron were at the dining room table relaxing with books and tea, listening to some old Shleu Shleu records. I had them all to myself and I started with my thoughts organized, but when the words came out of my mouth they sounded like paper shuffling.

"So, I could be getting a job this summer. Like, a real job in a real place."

Mary Moses looked up plainly from her book. Uncle Aaron's eyebrows arched up and he folded his pen into his notebook. They both waited for me to continue.

"I'm going to work at Souche. They're looking for a commis and…"

"That's a good summer job, Olive. You're an excellent cook already. You could probably teach them a few things."

I twisted my foot and picked at my nails.

"Yeah, they said they can take me now. Like, I could start right away. Five days a week."

"What is right away? Don't you have final exams coming up soon?"

"I was thinking of letting that go, Mamou. They can have me start at the restaurant as of this weekend."

"So you're giving up your classes?"

It wasn't really a question. Her face didn't move but her lips pressed into a tight line. There had been a scene like this before. My mother had decided that instead of going for an Early Childhood Education degree to eventually become a teacher, she was going to major in Theater Arts because she wanted to be an actress. That day Grandma Hélène had spent hours moaning, tucking her hair behind her ears, and wringing her hands at the news. She had pleaded with my mother to reconsider and study something that would give her more security, more respect. To Haitians, acting was not a profession. It was barely considered a decent extra curricular activity for girls of breeding and it was a calamity to hear that my mother was going to pass up the opportunity to study something of value, especially in this country where even though they had been there for over ten years, they were still randomly seen as refugees. They didn't have much money and their English was still a bit heavy, but Carly was as strong willed as her father had been, and my grandmother's voice never seemed to rise higher than a cat's meow.

Mary Moses had gone to my mother's recitals and shows when she was still in New York. She remembered sitting in the audience and watching her little sister send off sparks like lightning harnessed in a spotlight on stage. She knew Carly was good. She knew that she had a chance to actually make a good living, maybe even be a star. She also knew that her little sister was one to walk barefoot on an open road without looking down for glass.

When they were grown, Marie Lourdes wasn't able to watch over her sister like when they were girls. She married Aaron, an assistant professor who had just sold a manuscript to a publishing house in Québec, and they moved north to start his career while he taught at a University. Marie Lourdes went to nursing school and found a job at the General Hospital in Montréal. She wasn't around anymore to counsel her sister and argue with her about how her new lifestyle would affect her little daughter. She wasn't there to order her home after shows instead of going to another cast party. She wasn't there to smell the alcohol on her breath and the marijuana in her hair and shake some sense into her before things got out of hand.

I imagine that after all the lost years, the hurt of losing her sister was still sharp in her heart and made her hold the children in the pediatric intensive care unit with an extra bit of care than she was required to give. Maybe she told herself that saving babies was a forward payment made in Carly's name. Those thoughts faded and Mary Moses' temperature rose while she looked at me shifting my weight and chewing my lip. My words floated up like steam evaporating over a boiling pot.

"How will you start classes at the university in the fall? You said you wanted to go for the Communications program. Your uncle made sure you have a spot. What about that?"

"Mamou, I feel like I understand food best and I want to learn how to be great at it right on the job."

"So, you would want to be a chef?" Uncle Aaron was always trying to soften things.

"Yes, uncle."

"Even if that is what you want to do, you don't simply show up and say you're a chef! You must go to culinary school, you have to learn!"

Mary Moses's tone was turning rough. "You don't just show up and say you're Julia Child and they take you! This is not a television show we are living in."

"You know I'm good. The owner gave me a test

and he says I have talent..."

"A test? What kind of test? In the back of the
kitchen somewhere? Ah! This is ridiculous..."

"I know what I'm doing!" It was the first time
that I had ever raised my voice in the slightest to
Mary Moses. It turned my intention into a piercing
challenge. Flames rose in her little eyes and the
room became stifling.

"So you are grown then? You are doing what
you want?"

"Mamou..."

"No, no, no. You go do what you want.
Obviously there's no stopping you. But you will
choose. You take this job and you go learn. But I
never want to hear a single word about the hours,
about how demanding the chef is, or about the
shitty pay. I want to see results. You hear me?"

"Results?"

"Yes!" She pounded her first on the table.

"You say you want to be a chef? I want to see it
happen. You pick a day, once a week you will cook
dinner here and pay for every ingredient you use.
You will not waste my time or my energy."

I was too dumbfounded to answer. Mary Moses
had her hand balled into a fist on the table and
Uncle Aaron reached over to gently cover it. Her
breathing calmed, but she did not take back her

words. After two months of preparing meals with trembling hands and dark circles under my eyes, I packed my things and moved out.

∽✦∾

The following years were a blur. I don't know how I appeared to anyone else, but I know I became unrecognizable even to myself. I lived in Aziza's dorm room for two years and we got a ratty studio downtown when she graduated. It was surprisingly easy to go unnoticed by the residence staff. My work shifts at the restaurant were long and I didn't have anything but my clothes to move around. By then Ziz and I had our way of saying things without saying them, and by the third night that I crashed in her room, it was clear that I needed to stay. I didn't go home often, and after a while I stopped going altogether. There were too many stories flying around the Haitian network of family friends who always mean well but can't stop talking about your misfortune as though hearing it out loud would protect them from suffering the same fate.

The stories stacked themselves like soggy newspapers at Mary Moses' doorstep and there was no way to distinguish which one was real and which was total exaggeration. Someone had heard about me being dragged out of a bar by the police for disturbing the peace, screaming in the street. Someone else had seen me squatting to pee between cars near the bus terminal early one morning, just before rush hour. Yet another source reported that they had seen me hand cash to a man at the back entrance of the restaurant in exchange for something small that I shoved into my purse, looking over my shoulder. People were always repeating some piece of gossip that they thought Mary Moses needed to know until she started hanging up the phone the moment they mentioned my name.

A few years in, when I was a junior sous-chef at a nice place in the downtown area, one of my favorite things to do between the madness of prepping and checking the line was people watch. The house music that piped through the surround system barely matched the ambient murmur of voices so that people could still hear each other talk. I'd peek through the window in the metal door that led to the kitchen and looked at couples eating without looking at each other's faces, groups of girls talking over plates of food they didn't touch, fancy ladies with huge sunglasses savoring small bites and repeatedly asking the waiter to give their compliments to the chef. Then there were those blank faces, sometimes male, sometimes female, sometimes something in between, that came in and without looking at the menu ordered very specific items prepared in a very specific way. Local club performers came in wearing cheap jewelry and expensive leather. They tried to mix with the upscale clientele, but everyone in there had the same dirt under their fingernails, manicured or not.

One night a trio of leggy amazons came in hiding behind dark shades. They asked for a booth in the back and had the cash to make it happen before the hostess could run the spiel about those spots being "reserved." They ordered bourbon cocktails with appetizers and whispered together like international spies plotting a fashion takeover. The one with the platinum blonde beehive wig kept her glasses on and used her napkin to dab her eyes and blow her runny nose. I pumped the server for info and it turns out the sick one was the choreographer and the other two were back up singers for Tina Turner. She was in town for the next two nights on her 24/7 tour and there was no room for anyone sick.

When the server came in to pick up their second round of cocktails, I added a shot glass of something for the sick one, on the house. When the server came back with the shot, I adjusted my white cap and put on a clean apron. I checked my makeup and walked out to the booth with the shot on a small silver platter.

"Really? What's this?" One of the other two amazons chuckled and crossed her legs.

"We're just trying to relax, but thank you…"

"Of course, ladies. I appreciate the pressure to perform under challenging circumstances. I just wanted to share a bit of something homemade I use when I can't take my glasses off. I assure you it works every time."

I set the platter down and walked away. I didn't look back and I didn't ask the server about them at the end of the night. But the next night, I did get a gift basket with all sorts of girly goodies like candles, a vibrator, fancy makeup, and a bottle of bourbon, with a card signed by the Acid Queen herself.

The next thing I knew, musicians, road managers, producers, and opening acts were randomly making stops at the restaurant for a little something that apparently couldn't be found anywhere else. I slid into another level of the Montréal nightlife scene that really only got kicking after most eateries closed and didn't stop until the sun came up. I was snorting cocaine every other day and didn't see a reason to stop. My boss thought I was amazing, my crew thought I was cool, and over time I was being sought after for talents that went from serving food to serving other things that nourished just as well. That's what the word was anyway. But not everyone knew who I was. After all, I wasn't the Executive Chef, and I spent most of my time behind the scenes.

One look is all it took for me, though. I was holding the door open for the steward, dictating special order items when I saw him following the host to a booth at the far left were it was dim.

"Hey, Maxo. C'mere." I stopped a server as he adjusted his collar and hitched his pants.

"Yes, Chef Ollie?"

"Which section are you working tonight?"

"The front left, VIP."

"OK. Tip top, all right? We might have a critic in the house."

"Ugh. Who is it?"

"Just be sharp and come straight to me if there's anything, OK?"

"Yes, will do."

I felt pins and needles in my fingertips. Suddenly my jacket was two sizes too big and I couldn't adjust. Something was pulsing from my heart through every connecting blood vessel all over my body. I went to the back of the kitchen and pressed my hot hands flat on the stainless steel counter. After ten breaths, I turned on the cold water and let it run over my wrists. The more it ran, the clearer it became. I could hear small soft voices muffled by the rustle of brown paper bags. I could see Mary Moses' garden clearly, the placement of her rosemary, her mint, her daffodils, her wolfsbane, the tiny roots of all the different plants she grew curling down into the soil, reaching for each other, talking to each other, whispering a name.

∂∞∂

The next time I went home, five years after that last Christmas, it was a different house. All the rooms had been remodeled. The new style was glass, black and white floor tile and wireless equipment. The pictures on the walls had changed from gap-toothed grins on bikes to graduation poses and vacation snapshots, but I couldn't find myself in any of them. The boys had long since moved away. Peter was at university in Vancouver and Jude was living with his girlfriend in Toronto. The old-fashioned school desk that used to be in Peter's room was now in the front hall, and Jude's old BMX bike, all rusted, was leaning against the tool shed in the yard; but there was not one sign of me. As I moved cautiously down the hall, the sound of Coupé Cloué's voice floating from the speakers was thankfully familiar.

I followed the breeze coming in from the open patio door and went into the kitchen. It too had been updated with a dishwasher, a double-door refrigerator that gave ice and filtered water with the push of a button, and cabinets with straight stainless steel handles. It all looked brand new, with almost no trace of the old smells. There was a bowl of lemons on one end of the counter and a garland of fresh garlic hanging near the windowsill. On the other end was the wooden mortar and pestle, the *pilon* Mary Moses had taught me how to mash spices in. I brought it to my nose and closed my eyes. It was faint, but it still smelled like love. There was a shuffle upstairs, then the sound of a door closing.

"Hello? Is anyone home?"

"Who's there?" From upstairs, Uncle Aaron's voice didn't sound particularly worried. I hardly knew how to answer. To say *me* would be too presumptuous. I hadn't been me in that house for years. I was actually surprised that my key still worked.

"*C'est moi.* It's Olive."

He came down the stairs and beamed as soon as he saw me.

"Hey! It's my girl! Ah, come to me!" Uncle Aaron pulled me into his chest in the same rough way he always had when I was a teenager. He used to pat my head and rub my face almost like a dog and I'd squirm to keep him from messing up my hair or smudging my make up. This time I let him squeeze me as hard as he wanted and sway us back and forth. I peeked over his shoulder at the stairs, but there was no one coming down after him. He released his embrace and held me by my elbows. He stared into my face, inspecting it for traces of damage, any evidence of a further fall. But there was none. In fact I looked better than I had in a long time. I'd gained a little weight and my skin was clear.

"Yeah, I'm an old broad, Uncle. I have some gray hair now, y'know!"

"Old broad? Ha! *Ma petite Olive.* You're always the same to me. Come, come."

We sat at a counter that replaced the kitchen table where we all used to have breakfast. Now it was a fancy dark granite peninsula.

"How are you, my girl?"

"I'm good. Head chef now."

"Really? At the same place?"

"No, no, I left Souche a long time ago."

"Ah, ok. So you're well? Everything is all right?"

I knew what he was asking, trying to be discreet, trying to avoid anything upsetting.

"Everything is fine, uncle. Uncle, I…"

In one motion, he ran his heavy hand over my face sweeping from my forehead down to my chin, wiping away my words before they could come out.

"Shhh…"

I don't know if he knew what I wanted to say. Maybe he could feel that whatever was edging itself up my throat would hurt me in the telling more than it would hurt him. Maybe it wasn't the right time yet, and maybe he knew that. He knew that in spite of everything, it would never be the right time to say, but he loved me anyway. He pulled me into another embrace that made me feel like a rescued child again and I almost allowed myself that relief. I let my head lean on his shoulder and closed my eyes to breathe. Then I heard the floor creak above us and realized that Mary Moses was definitely not going to come down.

I imagined her face. The dark eyes that had stayed placid all those years ago at the sight of my broken body were now hidden from me. I could only picture her now sitting in her room, irritated at her husband for receiving me so warmly after everything. After what I had done. He had always been the softer one, the one who was inclined to offer another chance when any of us did something wrong. Mary Moses' character had been forged in flames and for better or for worse, there was always a point beyond which she would not bend. I knew she was still angry that I had fallen so far from her protection. She had tried to make me into something better than what I came from, but she had failed. I fell down the same rabbit hole that had claimed her sister's life, and though it seemed I had survived the fall, my own transgression was unforgivable.

"I went away for a while. I took some time and... And, anyway, I wanted to tell you guys that I'm leaving for good. I'm going back to New York."

"Oh? Did you find a good position there?"

"I'm opening my own restaurant."

"Really? That's wonderful, Ollie! I hoped you would end up doing that sooner or later."

I shook my head at his enthusiasm that never doubted anything we ever said we wanted to do. I could have told him that I was going to build a house on the moon and he would smile and tell me he would buy a telescope so he could wave to me at night. He never needed the logistics for our dreams, he was just happy we had them.

"And there's also this." I took an envelope out of my purse and placed it on the counter in front of him. He just looked at it, almost waiting for the heavy cream paper and gold calligraphy to start talking.

"Open it."

He unfolded the invitation and I watched his eyebrows dance with a million questions.

"Marriage?"

"Yup."

He patted his chest pocket for his glasses. When he didn't find them, he squinted and pulled the card further away from his face.

"Araya. That's not American, is it?"

"His father is Spanish and his mother is Swedish, but they're all from Switzerland and they speak French. It's really complicated."

"Ah. So, I'm losing you to Europeans, *hein*?"

"I'm only going to New York, Uncle. It's not that far away. Besides, it's not like we really see each other now anyway." It wasn't a reproach, more of a sad fact. He shrugged and tilted his head to look at me.

"Still. I never thought it would be this hard to let you go."

Uncle Aaron suddenly looked tired. His salt and pepper hair was cut short and his skin was still supple, but there were bags under his brown eyes. The stubble on his chin was white and gruff. I didn't want to look at him, I didn't want to start crying. My voice could barely come out.

"Uncle, you can never lose me."

"I know I'm not your father, Olive. I always knew I could never take his place. I stood back and let your aunt make all decisions about you. But, you know... you have always been my girl."

I turned to face the window. A pounding started behind my eye and it was hard to breathe from the tears blocking my throat. I stood up and almost knocked over my chair.

"Ok, well, I should go now. I'm flying this evening and I still have some things to pack."

"Ok, baby."

We walked arm in arm to the door and hugged again in a wordless goodbye. I looked at the ceiling, wondering which room Mary Moses was in.

❧

On the morning of my wedding, the view from the back terrace of the Peach Grove Inn was like a postcard. Hills rolled on in varying shades of green out to the horizon to meet a clear blue sky. About a mile off, a wooden fence kept a few brown horses from wandering into a neighboring meadow that belonged to an apple orchard. A wide weeping willow in the yard made the perfect altar. The wedding coordinator, a busty blonde dressed in a tuxedo, made sure every moment was going according to a precise schedule. She had a stopwatch hanging around her neck and rushed around giving hand signals to her crew like they were on a television set.

Every room in the Greek revival bed and breakfast was appointed with some measure of lace and potpourri. A silver candelabrum with tall white tapers sat on a doily on the baby grand piano in the sitting room. The chandelier at the front entrance caught the mid-morning sun and sent little rainbow flecks all over the walls and the floor. The carved banisters were wound with white silk ribbon and there were floral arrangements at the landings. The owners of the place stayed out of the way in their private quarters and only came out when the coordinator had a question about where she could tuck the garden hose or how far the nearest drugstore was. It was springtime and there wasn't a cloud anywhere, but there was a tent set up anyway arranged with white chairs in neat formation under it. There was no harm in being prepared for rain.

When it was finally time to start, I breathed in the scent of white lilies that seemed to be everywhere: in bouquets on the landings, floating in a bowl on the dining table, hanging in an arch over the doorway. Loose curled petals made a trail from the back steps out to the yard. They traced an aisle leading up to the Justice of the Peace and my future husband poised under the sad hanging branches of the willow. The DJ was hunched over with his ear pressed against his shoulder cueing my march music, the bartenders had lined up the bottles of champagne that they would pop and start pouring one after the other right after the ceremony ended. The photographer was snapping candid shots of the guests as they kept turning towards the stairs waiting to catch the first glimpse of my walk down into the whispering crowd. The two o'clock sun had warmed the air enough for people to start fanning themselves, but my eyes were still as a lake in winter.

"Dear friends,

We are gathered this day to celebrate the marriage of Olive Séraphin and Maximilian Araya. Marriage is the promise between two people who love each other, who trust each other, who honor one another as individuals and wish to spend the rest of their lives in partnership. It enables the two separate souls to share their desires, longings, dreams, joys and sorrows, and to help each other through all uncertainties of life..."

While the Justice of the Peace repeated the words he prepared for our ceremony, I was thinking about Love's Promise sitting on a table, uncollected. I never got a response to the invitation I had left with Uncle Aaron. Though I didn't have any indication that they would show up, I still ordered two dozen bulbs from a fancy nursery in Suffolk County that served all those wealthy summer homes and had them shipped to the inn so that I could present them to Mary Moses and Uncle Aaron after the ceremony. I knew they already had a few varieties in the front yard at the house, but these were special. They were the same ones that grew around Grandma Hélène's house in Haiti that was lost in that terrible fire all those years ago.

I wrapped the bulbs, still protected in their heavy plastic packing, in a yard of green linen tied with white silk ribbon. I was going to walk up to Mary Moses and Uncle Aaron with my new husband after exchanging vows and present them with my gift. They would be the first people we would address as a couple. That was my wish. That's how I imagined it would be.

When my groom slipped his ring onto my finger I scanned the front row, (hoping against hope), but the two seats I had reserved next to my mother were occupied by Aunt Madeleine and her partner Liliana. The music started back up, everyone clapped, and my gift stayed untouched on a small round table in a corner of the tent. Everyone admired the strange, beautifully wrapped package and asked about it. I smiled and explained what it was, that it symbolized growth, renewal, and love. The *oohs* and *ahhs* floated up in congratulations for something so thoughtful. I'm just glad no one asked who it was from, because I would have choked on the lump in my throat as I made up a lie.

My husband led me onto the dance floor and we started a slow glide to Donny Hathaway's "A Song for You." It's not really the kind of song you dance to. There's no consistent flow of rhythm that allows for dance moves, so we just swayed and twirled awkwardly. Our guests crowded around us in a circle that rolled by like a carousel. As we turned and turned, I still searched the smiling faces for the ones I needed to see, but they were definitely not there. At the end of the song we bowed like performers in a play. We smiled at everyone clapping and dabbing their eyes, and then I saw them. I lost my breath and immediately felt the sting of tears. Everyone was cheering, happy, and all sound fell away. I rushed toward them, dragging my husband behind me, stuttering introductions, and they pulled me into their arms as I cried. It was a tender moment to everyone watching us, because they didn't know what they were seeing.

"Congratulations, love."

"Thank you so much for coming, guys."

Jude and Peter took turns wiping my cheeks and pushing the veil back from my shoulders like I was the baby sister and not the oldest. My new husband turned into a piece of furniture at my elbow. Cameras flashed all around us as we held hands.

"So. Nothing?"

"You know she loves you, Ollie. It's just... What can I tell you? When the Chief digs her heels in, that's it."

"I know. It's okay, Pete. You don't have to say any more. I'm just so happy you guys are here."

We hugged again and I gave an exaggerated smile to cover my heartbreak. A server passed with a platter of champagne glasses but I didn't want alcohol to dilute the moment.

"Ollie, look. I have a little something for you." Jude reached into his jacket pocket and took out his wallet.

"Are you kidding me? Are you seriously trying to give me money? *Judee*, get outta here!"

I laughed and wanted to slap the wallet out of his hands. There wasn't a gift he could give me that would make me happier than seeing them at my wedding, or that would soothe the hurt of their parents not being there. I started curling my lips to say something sarcastic, but then Jude pulled out a small picture that was tucked in the space behind the business cards and the cash. There was a deep crease mark from where it was folded over and the color had turned sepia from years of being layered between the leather. He smoothed it out and put it in my hand. It was us: Mary Moses, Uncle Aaron, Peter, Jude, and me on the day we had gone to a photographer's studio to take a family portrait. I was a skinny thirteen, and my huge head looked like it barely balanced on my scrawny neck, but I was smiling. My skin was still a little pale and my puff-sleeved dress looked a bit childish for my height, but I was showing my teeth, which was rare. We were huddled in a group embrace the photographer encouraged and we had all said cheese when he asked us to. In spite of the corniness, our smiles were real and we were happy. Another tear rolled down and dropped from the tip of my nose and splashed onto our faces. Jude let me hold the picture a little while longer then gently took it from me. He folded it back into his wallet like it was an ancient papyrus. Cameras clicked as we embraced.

6 Aziza

The morning of my wedding, I sipped bourbon from a teacup and sat in a tufted Chippendale chair by the window of my room at the Peach Grove Inn. The sun filtered through the lace curtains, giving just the right light for putting on armor. Some smooth R&B floated out of an iPod on the bed. I closed my eyes and leaned forward to give Aziza my face. She cupped my chin with a firm hand and tilted my head back. Her steady breath fell in a murmur of secrets that melted into my skin. Her fingers dipped into jars of cream foundation and fluttered over a palette of shadows and blush. She had lip liner, gloss, sticks of kohl, and wands of mascara in a leather case that she had brought in like a box of ammunition. Her hands worked quickly, reaching back and forth instinctively for the right brush or sponge.

"I didn't even like you at first. Did you know that?" I asked.

"Bitch, please. I couldn't stand _you_."

"What? Why? Why didn't you like me?" I opened my eyes wide waiting for her answer. Aziza just shifted on her hip and kept working. Her red lips curved up in a gangster lean.

"Well?" I cocked my head and she tapped my nose with the tip of a bronzer brush.

"Oh, who the hell knows? You sure tamed me, didn't you?"

The girl was amazing. She played varsity basketball in high-top sneakers and twisted up her endless mass of curly hair in a velvet scrunchie for gym class. She had hairy forearms, a uni-brow, and a smile that made you feel like you choose the wrong outfit for everything. In the beginning, we stayed aloof in that silly way that girls snub each other without any real cause. She'd catch me sneering over at her in the cafeteria just as she was shoveling a forkful of spaghetti into her mouth. She'd stand steps away from my locker giggling with a classmate she had no interest in just to make sure I noticed her, then she'd ignore me when I passed by. I don't remember our first conversation, but I know that at some point we locked eyes and I recognized her heart like I recognize the freckles on my own face.

Aziza held my gown open for me to step into. She zipped me up, surveyed the fall of the fabric just past my heels and pursed her lips in approval. She snapped a tiny stone on the enclosure for my something blue, and hung a huge diamond family heirloom around my neck for my something borrowed. There were new things, like my engagement ring and the strappy white shoes that she secured for me so I wouldn't mess up my nails. And there were old things, like the hurts that tagged us both with scars. A small bump from a broken nose for her. A long centipede-shaped line on my elbow for me. Those marks replaced sentimental terms like 'best friend' or 'sister' and took away the need for any mushy words in this moment of preparation. Aziza put the finishing touches on my war paint and I didn't look in the mirror once. I trusted my friend's skills completely. I knew she earned them long ago from another warrior on another battlefield.

༰ལྦ

When she was about five, Aziza and her mother ran into the bathroom and huddled together on a pile of towels behind the locked door. They stayed there while her father banged on the other side screaming slurred, threatening words. They waited until the door stopped rattling and his ranting voice trailed off to the bedroom where he would invariably fall asleep. When they uncurled from each other, Aziza and her mother stood up and looked at their reflections in the mirror that took up the whole wall. Her heart was still pounding as she watched her mother wipe her face with a cold washcloth and rearrange her hair. They were expecting dinner guests in a little over an hour, and she could never answer the door showing that face. Fortunately, she knew how to create another one.

She took out her pouch full of cosmetics that was full set of brushes, pencils, jars, pots, and sticks, and layered on a new attitude. Fresh foundation covered three-day-old bruises and loose powder camouflaged the redness of that afternoon's attack. The heavy black line around her eyes distracted from the swelling under them. The pewter and gold tones in the shadow made her brown eyes glow and the layers of mascara gave them back their sensuous veil. A tiny brush styled her brows to a stately frame. Another dusting of powder, light blush. For the lips it was a creamy neutral so as not to distract from the eyes. It was always the eyes. She knew that one look could reveal everything while obscuring it all at the same time, and her talents were strong on that fine line. She clipped on a pair of simple gold earrings and gently repaired her curls with wet fingers. She smoothed Aziza's hair and wiped her small face without a word. She took a deep breath and opened the bathroom door. Together they crept past the bedroom and saw that he was asleep.

By the time company arrived, he would come downstairs smelling of cologne and mouthwash, mumbling something charming about taking longer to get ready than his beautiful wife. Their guests would laugh and settle into the living room, nibble on the hors d'oeuvres arrayed on the coffee table. They would all laugh, enjoy drinks and dinner, have a lovely night. But as Aziza sat, prim and quiet on the sofa, watching the adults, her soft skin crawled with heat. Her little heart stewed in bubbling anger.

As she got older, it was always just under the surface and sputtered out in her haughty tone, in her hard gaze, and in her sharp words. She didn't really want to be so cutting. She wanted to be soft and nurturing like her mother, but that was too tall of an order. She randomly got in trouble in elementary school for yelling at a teacher or for scrapping in the schoolyard with kids older than her. Most of the time it was in defense of someone else; some kid she didn't even know that well. She was a middle school superhero looking to squash evil wherever it reared its ugly face, or maybe it was the constant storm in her that needed a convenient place to rain down on to keep it from suffocating her.

At home, she stalked around the house, carefully avoiding the creaks under the rugs, so no sound would interfere with the murmured voices of her parents in their room. She couldn't always tell right away if they were sounds of love or of conflict. She'd listen for a thunderous crack followed by furniture tumbling or glass shattering. She'd pause on the stairs or in the hall, holding her breath, waiting, listening. Even when minutes passed and the decibel didn't rise, she'd tiptoe to her room and bundle herself in her bed with her face pressed against the pillow soaking up angry tears.

Early one morning, when Aziza was headed out for an early study group on campus, she stopped in the kitchen and found her mother sitting at the table sipping tea. Her legs were crossed at the ankle and her robe was tied with the sleeves neatly cuffed. She hadn't turned on the light but the spring daybreak had already flooded the room.

"Ma, what are you doing?"

"Your father went to the office early. You want tea?" Her voice was calm and her eyes were still. She ran her fingers through her hair from her forehead to nape of her neck and turned her bare face up to her daughter.

"*La, shukraan.* I'm good."

Aziza looked in her mother's eyes and noticed for the first time how calm they were. For once she wasn't wearing any make up so there was nothing to camouflage her expression. In this clean light, Aziza could see a peace in her mother that couldn't be swayed by fear or anger, or anything. It was deliberate. Aziza observed how she commanded the rise and fall of her brows, of her cheeks, of the corners of her lips. The soft lines around her eyes could tell more stories that her mouth ever would, and even they did not reveal anything. As Aziza read her mother's face, the temper that constantly simmered on her own momentarily dissipated. She sat down and slid her hand across the table.

"You're getting an early start also," her mother said. "Exams coming up?"

"Ma. Why are you still here?"

"What do you mean still? Where am I going?"

"Why do you stay here? With him? Assad and I are not babies anymore. There's no reason for you to keep surviving this."

She prayed for an answer that would make sense, one that would validate the violence that spilled out of her during arguments with her younger brother, altercations on campus, snarling at a cashier or at a gas station attendant. Everywhere but at home. There, it stayed sealed under glass as she took cues, smiled, kissed on both cheeks. It lay in waiting for a hurricane to smash everything with a devastating hand that would send the walls and the roof and all the windows caving in to free her, her mother and brother from the cage they were in. She kept waiting for a getaway plan complete with duffle bags, wool caps, and Greyhound bus tickets like in the movies. Her mother took a sip of tea and gave a slow blink.

"There are monsters everywhere, *habibi*. It doesn't matter where you go."

Aziza had no response. The petulance she would have normally bounced back with stalled in her throat. She looked at her mother calmly holding her cup and suddenly felt a softness she didn't want. There was a resignation that she didn't welcome, and an amnesty she would continue to refuse. She had started coming home later and later every day, and spraying herself with free perfume samples from department stores before she crept in the door. She washed her hair several times a week to erase the funk from the cheap marijuana she got from a guy on campus. When she couldn't find him, she sometimes got it from the ratty goths who seemed to major in nothing other than makeup application and moping. At night she'd stand under the shower until her fingers were deeply pruned and she felt heavy with water, but it wasn't enough. There had to be something more to keep her from smashing her fist through the shower door or into the mirror in her room. Or into her father's face.

∂∽⊸

I could hear the activity on the other side of my door. People were rushing in and out of rooms looking for boutonnieres or a bottle of clear nail polish, going for an extra swipe of deodorant, shaking hairspray cans. It was quiet in my room. I tucked a curl that had escaped a bobby pin. Aziza dusted bronzer on my bare shoulders. I dabbed perfume on my wrists and in the crook of my elbows. She secured the veil into my hair with clips. I adjusted my earrings. She checked the clasp on my bracelet. Everything was in its place. She took my trembling hands and wound our fingers together. This was our last moment before battle.

"Ready?"

I looked at my white knuckles, then locked eyes with my friend.

"Ready."

She opened the door and we joined the bridal party gathered in the hall. They were all wide-eyed and smiling, gasping in admiration and showering me with singsong compliments. Their hands reached to fluff the veil down my back and inspect the ribbon on my bouquet. Aziza was the only one who wasn't beaming. She gave me the solemn look of a Samurai going into certain death with shoulders back and eyes resigned. She watched me in my regalia as I went down the stairs toward my fate.

The seats were lined up with military precision in eight equal rows on either side of the aisle. Every guest was fittingly dressed and coiffed for the occasion, but I couldn't tell who was an ally and who was an enemy. The wedding march played and a collective gasp rose up like arms to carry me along; numbness draped over me like my veil. As I walked on, careful not to let my heels sink into the earth, I had the feeling that I didn't know where I was going. By the time I made it to the willow tree, I had walked a million miles and I was lost. The quiet spread around me like rapids that kept growing and turning, curling into hundreds of new currents rising and parting unexpectedly into steady pools that promised the way to safety, but they really led nowhere.

❦

We had both smoked weed for years already, since high school. We used to stand in a huddle behind the school with some kids while a cheap blunt got passed around. By the time it got to me the tip was always moist and I hated the idea of sucking on someone else's spit, so I dragged heavy and quick. I passed it on and when it got to Ziz, she'd pull way too hard and break out into a coughing fit. Everyone laughed at her clutching her chest and wiping her runny eyes.

I listened to her talk for hours and understood that it was my job to analyze her high rantings whenever she had them. In between the eye drops, perfume sprays, and popping Altoids, smoking weed became as regular to us as a cigarette smoker pulling out their Du Maurier Lights at a bus stop. She talked a lot, mostly complaining about men. What they did, what they didn't understand, how she imagined castrating a few of them with her teeth. I think I was a good listener, but after a while, depending on what the latest crisis was, it was clear that we were both looking for something more to get us through the pause between our dramas. I was looking for a hard push, while she needed to calm the hell down.

I'd lost sight of her for a little while at one of our regular late-night spots when the music got louder and the lights got even dimmer. She came floating out of the bathroom and eased onto the couch next to me. Her hands settled softly on the glass table, then on my shoulder, then on her own face. She took my hand and guided my fingers to touch the tears that rolled from her eyes as she smiled.

"Ollie. Ollie. *Ollie Ollie oxen freeee…*"

All the knots had loosened and the sharp points had been smoothed. Her usual triggers disappeared and nothing was wrong. She was slow and liquid. I could tell that she had just done something more than weed, but I didn't know what. When I found out that it was heroin, it was too late to go back. I took her in my arms and pushed her curls away from her face. She cuddled against me like a child and smeared makeup on my blouse. One of her shoes fell off as she brought her leg across my lap. I gathered her knees together and pulled them in to me.

"We're okay, babe. It's fine."

"One two three… Red light, green light, one two three." Her voice trailed then stuttered into giggles.

"Ok. You're green, and I'm red. Go and stop, stop and go."

The music changed to a deep house groove and she started flicking her wrist in the air with her face still pressed against my chest. Our friends followed suit and danced around us flicking their wrists and tossing their hips to the rhythm. Red light/Green light became our code. If she pulled out an A-Bomb, I'd chill in the cut with some cocktails and cigarettes. Just easy. Even inebriated, I could control my senses enough to pull her back onto the curb when the taxis were whizzing by with no intention of stopping. I could stay cool enough to shield her from an agitated barfly who was trying to get a rise out of her. Someone was always trying to get a rise out of my Ziz. I think they could tell that even though she was sedated, she was ready to explode into fireworks with the right spark. And that could still be fun.

On the nights when I took out my silk pouch and glass straw, she knew to stick to weed in case she had to step in between me and a bitch wearing too much makeup and food stains on her shirt who didn't know when it was time to go home. But we never went home. There was no real home. The apartment we shared at that time was spacious, on the second floor of a nice building. No doorman, but still nice. It was a place to sleep and clean our wounds before facing the world again. We took our drugs and did all we could do to hide from being grownups, but it was just running as fast as we could toward a light that invariably blinded us when we finally opened our eyes.

"Ollie! You up?"

The sun was high and pouring in through all the windows in our apartment. Ziz usually kept the heavy curtains in her bedroom drawn to keep out the light so she could sleep in on weekends, but when she shuffled out to the kitchen it was everywhere and she shielded her crumpled face.

"Ollie! It's noon already, I know you're not still sleeping?"

She lit a low flame under the kettle and came dragging into my room.

"Well, don't you look lovely?"

"Shut up. Make me some of your tea, please? I'm going by my parents later and I need to be ready for the firing squad. I put the kettle on already."
She plopped onto my bed and wiggled up to the pillow next to me.

"Jeeze, you're frickin' wide awake. Did you sleep at all?" Ziz yawned like a baboon. "What's wrong?"
All I could do was stare at my friend. I was dropping a telepathic bomb full of words I wanted to say but couldn't. She saw the twitch in my cheek and felt it right away.

"Ollie, they said it had nothing to do with the food. The guy was probably already sick or something."

"I know what they said."

"So why'd you leave, then? Nobody said you had to leave."

"I couldn't stay there anymore, Ziz."

"Why?"
Aziza inched in closer, adjusting the pillow under her head. She pushed her curls away from her face, as if they were preventing her from hearing me.

"What is it?"

"I knew him."

"The guy who died? Was he a critic?"

I propped myself up on my elbows, but we were still close enough for me to feel her breath fall against my arm. The sheets and comforter covering my legs suddenly felt like they were made of lead. I stared straight ahead at my open bedroom door, out to the sunlight flooding the kitchen and the living room.

"Talk to me, Ollie."

"We would have never met, Ziz. You know that? I would be living a completely different life somewhere, every minute of it wanting to die. Dying. Or maybe already dead by now." Aziza's forehead furrowed, but she waited for me to continue.

"I barely escaped being dragged to hell. Not movie hell, or book hell. Real hell that you can't even imagine until it's reaching for you and you can't move and you piss yourself and you throw up from the smell of it. And it's touching you, breathing on you, and you can't even scream for help. I was almost ripped open by a demon, Ziz. A thing that grows bigger and stronger with every soul it takes.

"That man pimped my mother and had her fucked up on drugs. He had used kids before and had his eye on me. Can you imagine that, Ziz? A thing like that gets fatter and slimier with time, and it stays dirty no matter what it wears. If you know one, you can smell it as soon as it comes around. Even after so much time, when you meet that thing again, the thing that you tamed and that has tamed you, you're responsible for sending it home. Right?"

I was trembling and Aziza waited to be sure I was finished talking. We both listened to the kettle start to whistle and then scream without moving. With everything that we already knew about each other, there were still some stories that had stayed untouched, buried so far down that digging them up would only hurt more, to tell and to hear, so we left them where they were. But every now and then, a buried thing bursts out of the ground without warning and you just have no choice but to see it, hopefully not alone, and confess.

Ziz inched even closer to me. She wrapped her arms around my waist and hugged me tight. It wasn't really a consoling hug. It was desperate arms wrapped around a tree in hurricane winds, bracing against the whipping rain, holding breath through each deep roll of thunder.

"You belong to me now." She held me and didn't say another word.

❧

In the wee hours of our last Christmas morning together, Aziza and her latest man had a fight about something neither of them could remember. She had spent hours riding and was lounging in her bed trying to paint her nails, spilling red polish on her pillowcase, singing drowsily along with the Christmas carols floating out of the radio on her dresser. Her shoes were on the kitchen table and the refrigerator door was wide open. She had come home with Chinese takeout, but the paper bag from Fu-Ying still sat on the counter, stapled shut with the dark grease mark spreading across the bottom. She heard the buzzer, and sucked her teeth. She heard the banging on the window, but didn't get up. She heard glass smashing in the living room, but it didn't matter. She was already under water.

She looked up at him from where she lay on the edge of her bed with a soft glaze in her eyes, but there was something in his eyes, too. He had been drinking and was in no mood for refusals. He had lost his job just before the holiday season and needed to borrow money. She gave a groggy smile and apologized for the mess, but before she got a full sentence out he grabbed her by the shoulders and shook her like a rag doll. Her head bobbed in slow motion while she reached to wipe a stream of drool that was escaping her mouth. The latest man punched her in the chest, sending her face down against the cream rug by her bed. He stepped on her hand while he ransacked the room looking for her purse.

It was almost two in the morning and I was on my way back from seeing my family on the north shore. Haitians usually opened presents at midnight and partied until the wee hours, but when I left there was no party going on. I was upset, high on cocaine, and had no patience for the other cars on the road. I left them behind in zigzags of rock salt as I pressed my bare foot on the gas pedal. I had tried to call Aziza several times on the way, but never got an answer. I kept tearing down the highway and cut my turns so hard my wheels screeched and my whole body leaned to one side. When I got to our building, I parked too close to the car on my left and had to crawl out through the passenger side because I couldn't open my door.

I rushed through the lobby with my shoes in my hands and found him standing at the top of the stairwell shifting from foot to foot, eyes darting, sweating. I could smell the alcohol wafting down and could practically see it seeping from his pores.

He was blinking and twitching even more than I was. He knew that I was going to hurt him.

With my eyes locked on his I called Aziza's name, but she didn't answer. A door down the hall cracked open a little, but I already knew it was our old lady neighbor who made it her job to stay awake all night and constantly check on us wayward girls. Her door closed back again and locked. I called for my friend two more times, watching him pant like a cornered dog. In that moment I transformed into something I did not recognize. The everyday me— the one who cooked in a fancy restaurant every day, who cried at the movies, who chewed the inside of my cheek raw from nervousness—that me folded into a small compartment in the back of my brain. Another ferocious, not quite human me that roared instead of screamed, took over.

I dropped my purse and charged up the stairs like a linebacker, stepping high, two by two. I barreled my head into his stomach and sent us crashing into the wall then onto the floor. I straddled his chest and wailed my fists into his face, grunting like an animal, which made him screech like a woman. He finally grabbed my wrists and squeezed them so hard I thought my bones would snap between his fingers, but I was too high and too angry to be conquered.

I scraped my knees on the rough carpeting from squeezing my thighs against his ribs. I yanked my arms apart and hurled my head against his. Our skulls collided and I felt my skin split at the hairline. He let go of my wrists to cover his own gushing wound. With blood streaming down my face, I pounded my fists into his nose, his cheeks, his mouth. Each time my knuckles bashed into his flesh, I went in harder with another swing. I pulled back for the next wild punch and my elbow collided with the metal banister. I howled in pain as the impact tore my skin, spurting blood. He pushed me off him and spit out a few bloody teeth.

While I crouched against the wall glaring at him with my hair wild and my face bloody, I wasn't afraid that he'd come after me. Though I was injured, my eyes were feral with warning that he knew to heed. He slithered down the stairs and disappeared out the lobby door before the police sirens got too close.

The apartment door was open and I found Aziza on the floor of her room. We couldn't run anymore because there was no place left to go. The brick wall we kept slamming ourselves against had no sympathy for our broken bones and smashed insides. I knelt and pulled my friend upright and tried to check her neck for a pulse. I couldn't tell if I was feeling her heart, or my own, vibrating with adrenaline from the fight and the coke and the fear. I pressed my bloody face to hers to feel for breathing. I touched my lips to her nose, prepared to stop my own breath if I didn't find hers. She finally coughed without opening her eyes and I screamed in gratitude. I found my cell phone and called for an ambulance first. Then I called her mother.

I left Aziza in her hospital bed. I was cleaned up and stitched relatively quickly, but there was no telling how long she would lie with oxygen in her nose and an IV in her arm. They let me in to see her for a few minutes only, but then I had to leave the room. I roamed the halls and rode the elevator, stopping on every floor for half an hour until I had the courage to go to the waiting area to look for her mother. To tell her everything. To tell her the truth.

I kept picking at the bandage around my arm and couldn't push my voice past the knot in my throat. When I finally found her, she took my breath away. I hadn't seen her in years and I was amazed at how little she had changed. Her perfectly arched brows stayed still over deeply shadowed lids and lashes that hardly blinked. Her lips kept a resigned half smile while my words came tumbling out like boulders down the side of a mountain. Her back was straight and her hands stayed folded on her knees for a long time. But eventually, as I revealed more about how we'd been living, the more I stripped away Aziza's veneer, her mother's chin started to quiver. Her chest heaved slowly, and finally, tears rolled over the black rim of her eyes.

I couldn't feel the twenty stitches closing the gash on my elbow, or the five across my forehead. It was my throat that burned with guilt, but I explained and begged and swore between sobs until the words coming out of my mouth didn't make sense anymore.

"*Mami*, we had peanut butter and good bread...I bathed her, when she wouldn't wake up... salty grapefruit tea... that's what I knew...the oil, the oil you use in your hair that smells so nice... I never forgot the lights, red light, green light... but she was only a chipper anyway, nothing crazy... cause we have bills, everybody has bills y'know... but we did all right, it was all right... I know I should've..."

Aziza's mother lifted my chin. Her soft hands cupped my face and wiped the tears from my cheeks.

"Shhh, enough. It's ok. She'll be ok. I'll take care of her now. But you have to go away, *habibi*. For her

sake, and for your own. Go, and never come back
here   again."

7 My First Husband

The man I married was clean-shaven and kept his fingernails short, which I liked. Max had that untraceable accent people have when they speak five different languages fluently. His father was a famous Spanish architect and his mother was a Swedish maniac who drank wine for breakfast and constantly referred to the law degree she earned but never actually used. They had lived in Paris, but were really from Zurich, and landed in New York for a project his father was working on and ended up staying. He lived his life in chauffeured cars, cashmere pullovers, and pedigree. He had had a couple serious romances before me, but nothing that led to marriage, and no children. There was nothing about him to challenge my inexperience with a real relationship and I fell for the mirage that he was.

We met at an art show one summer night in Harlem where the walls were covered with skateboards and high-top sneakers. I guess he was slumming, looking for something cool to scuff his suede moccasins on. I had been clean for some years already and my hair was straight. I kept my makeup neutral, dressed in solid colors cut in simple lines, but maybe he saw the invisible ink on my clean slate. He knew he was bland, and maybe he could tell that I had the kind of edge that even after rehab, meditation, and hour-long showers, you could still smell. In that way, I guess we were a perfect match.

I walked right in to a routine with Max. Routine laughter. Routine posing for pictures in coordinating outfits. Routine touching in the same places with the properly timed moans. Routine responses to I want you, I love you, I miss you. Routine locking and un-locking of doors. I went along with our pantomime until I couldn't remember anymore how we had gotten there. Where was our first date? What did he say to get my phone number? Where did we honeymoon? Some beach somewhere. I didn't remember any of it. It was all a strange vague cloud that I hid in.

When he came into the restaurant with some friends and I made a show of coming out to serve him personally, patrons were always stunned to realize that he was my husband. When I periodically spent the day with him in his classroom, helping with runny noses, untied laces, and broken crayons, the other teachers were always wide-eyed that I was really his wife. It was sort of fun, because I liked the reactions. It was kind of like performing. But in another way it wasn't so fun; it was like the audience only came because they had to and the applause was half-hearted.

Two years into the marriage, my dear husband was staying out all night and coming home smelling more like scotch than his Paco Rabanne. He pretended it wasn't even happening and I never knew how to bring it up, so there were these heavy silences between us that we wore like clothes, keeping us from ever really being naked together. I told myself the story that we had a lifetime to nurture intimacy and that we'd get to understand each other better as the years rolled on. But he carried his cell phone in his pocket everywhere he went, even at home. He left me home alone to go on trips with his friends and I told myself I would not be one of those wives who crowded her husband and made him feel trapped by insisting he stay home all the time. I understood that despite the sentimental notion that we were now one, we were still two people with individual interests and we should be free to pursue them without restraint. I found ways to rationalize the empty wine bottles that piled in the compactor room every week. Who was I to judge him for going a little overboard with wine when I had been a full-blown coke head? How could I deprive him of his time with the fellas after dealing with little kids crawling all over him all day at work? I played the good wife. My job was to create the most comfortable environment possible to make my man glad that he had chosen me. Because isn't that what every woman wanted? To be chosen?

Between defending my frequent eating alone and having his friend Cory crash on our couch more nights than I liked, a stream of bitterness started to seep into every dish I prepared for dinner until he hardly ate at home anymore. I didn't stop cooking, though. It was my job, after all. It's one of the few jobs where bringing your work home was actually a good thing. But it didn't go over the way I expected it to. Our smiling friends were impressed with the dinner parties we threw. They brought wine and sweets and flowers, and I put my heart on the table. I always got applause and empty plates, but something was always missing, and my husband kept leaving our home to go find it. I expanded my repertoire and experimented with olives and feta and béchamel layered with ground beef and potato. I tried teriyaki with fresh ginger and blanched greens and clear noodles. I simmered lamb shanks with red lentils, cinnamon, turmeric, and cayenne. I prowled farmer's markets and gourmet shops like a sorcerer's apprentice picking out Marsala wine, chilies, chutneys, cumin seeds and coriander, but I still came up with nothing.

One day I was cleaning out my kitchen cabinets and I found the wooden mortar and pestle Mary Moses gave me when I was thirteen. I held it to my nose and breathed in deeply. I hadn't used it in years but I could still smell the old mix of garlic and scallions and thyme tattooed into the grain. I saw myself again standing in her kitchen soaking in the secrets that became my craft. I went back to what I knew. I sprinkled in ground black peppercorns and fat pinches of salt. I sliced garlic and Scotch Bonnet bulbs careful not to let my fingers touch the fiery seeds. I took hold of the pestle and ground ingredients together in steady, circular motions, mixing potions to feed the men who hungrily accepted what my darling husband left behind.

First it was Karl. They had met years before in Amsterdam on spring break. Karl had joined his friends in Europe and was astounded to find himself in a place where he could smoke weed freely and fuck as many white girls as he could without so much as a "please, baby, please." They met at a random house party when Karl had opened the door on my husband as he was taking a piss in the tub, the toilet seat being occupied by a guy with a girl balanced on his lap. Max became Karl's tour guide for the next week and they partied like old buddies. Karl ended up enrolling at ETH Faculty of Architecture in Zurich and moved back to New York after graduation. They lost touch for years, but when they bumped into each other at a concert in Madison Square Garden, they knew it was fated for them to stay friends.

At one of our regular dinner gatherings, Karl brought a date: a tall girl with her head shaved on one side and the other side draped in long sheets of golden hair. She wore a white sweater with matching leather pants, purple lipstick and perfume that was so strong I had to open a window to keep it from competing with the food. Every other man in the room, accompanied or not, stole glances at her, laughed at her jokes, wanted to know what she did for a living, tried to figure out the name of her fragrance; I bet they were imagining their tongues filling the gap between her two front teeth, or their cocks filling the gap between her skinny thighs. But as soon as dinner was served, the competition was over.

That night, it was a Puttanesca. I brought it out in a huge red pot that I set down in the middle of the table. The steam impatiently pushed its way out from under the lid and filtered up to hover over the table. There was already a platter of bread with olive oil and we moved the candles to make room. Some people like their Puttanesca paired with white rice, or laid over pasta. Others like it all by itself in a deep bowl so that it stays hot the whole time it's being eaten. I chose black, mushroom-flavored rice to be served on blue plates. The earthy, intimate aroma of the rice begged for my hot ragout to tangle itself with it.

As was the routine in our home, my husband sat at the head of the table and I was at the foot. I stood quietly in my place until everyone was watching, waiting, breathing in the magic that I was about to unveil. I picked up a potholder and a large serving spoon.

"Ladies and gentlemen, I present to you, Haitian Puttanesca. Or, as I like to call it, *Sos Bouzin*."

I lifted the lid. The motion of air being sucked in plugged everyone's ears and for a split second, they all went deaf. Time stood still as the aroma rose and spread steadily out. It floated, danced, and infiltrated every nose and throat at the table. I watched their eyes blink slowly and their lips slightly part. I went to get another spoon and when I came back, all hands held plates eager to be filled. I spooned a healthy dark mound of the mushroom rice onto the blue porcelain. It smoldered like a trembling volcano before I spread it into a circle. I plunged into the Puttanesca and poured heavy spoonfuls of it onto the rice. It was conch meat, firm to the tooth and tender to the tongue, blended in saucy harmony with crushed plum tomatoes, black olives, oyster mushrooms, white beans, garlic, onions and olive oil. The ingredients clung to each other, thick and lusty with tastes that whispered and screamed together at the same time. I smiled, handing the first plate ceremoniously to my husband. Then I moved faster, watching fingers wrap around fork handles. I served everyone with the same grace, but I saved Karl for last.

I watched his eyes move from my fingers to my spoon to my pot and back again. I watched his vision go double as he waited with his knees squeezed together, the muscles in his thighs taught and twitching. I had him.

He worked at a small private firm in Soho and kept unpredictably late hours. His team never knew when the lead architect was going to make a change to the design that would cause him to spend hours scrambling to update drawings to make a deadline. It was after ten when he called about two weeks after the dinner at our place. My husband was away at an overnight teacher's conference and would be home the next afternoon. Karl never even asked for his old running buddy. His voice was halting as he apologized for the late hour and he rambled on about propriety and respect, but I told him it was fine and that I understood perfectly. He said he had tried to make the Puttanesca, but it hadn't come out like mine. He wanted the recipe. He needed to know my secret ingredients so that he could try again, and perhaps have better luck.

"There's no secret at all. I'm happy to take you through it. When can you come by?" I said.

He came over the same night like a somnanbule, leaning forward in the doorway, almost on his toes, with his eyes dimmed and soft brown hair falling in a mess over his brow. I invited him into my kitchen and showed him everything he needed to know.

After Karl, there was Nick, the blond. Then Mason, the broad. Then Greg, the lean and hairless. After those friends, who weren't truly my husband's friends at all as it turns out, it was on to any man who was hungry.

෨⊷ை

Aziza tried to come see me whenever she had a layover New York. She was still based in Montreal, but it was like she had no home. She had long since let go of the apartment we had shared in Mile End and bought a condo in St. Laurent near her mother, but she was hardly ever there. Once she had more control of her schedule, she rented her apartment out to a young cousin at university for cheap. She crafted her time so that she was working constantly and moved from one hotel room to the next in Rio, Prague, Vancouver, Zurich, wherever. On vacations, she went to a beach somewhere or she came to New York to see me.

I'd go to her hotel room and we'd stay up talking like we were still in high school. She was clean, but she smoked cigarettes like crazy and to head off the toll from that habit (the cosmetic toll anyway), she had facials and teeth whitening on a regular basis. I begged her to stop smoking to keep away lung cancer and all, but she laughed at me. She said since heroin and alcohol hadn't managed to kill her, she'd take the Surgeon General's warning on her pack of DuMaurier lights as a friendly suggestion. She was never without her travel-sized toothpaste and toothbrush in her purse along with mints and tiny samples of her favorite perfumes. Aziza kept up a routine of Pilates and running that seemed to let the years and the damage of those years roll over her body without ever finding a place to park. It's like she was destined to look twenty-nine for the rest of her life and she swore to never have children because that was one gift she was unwilling to offer any man.

"I haven't been sleeping." I said.

"Nightmares?"

"Something like that. A scraggly little white man."

"Huh?"

"Cory. He crashes at our place every other week now, I swear."

"What are they, butt brothers or something?"

I rolled over to face Aziza, almost nose to nose. We couldn't have been more different. I was black and she was Middle Eastern, but we both had brown eyes and dark hair and big noses. We had stayed the same size since just after high school, even though her breasts were a bigger than mine and my butt was a bigger than hers. But if we put our hands up to touch, it was almost like looking into a mirror. Almost.

I could smell her last cigarette mixed with breath mints and the Narciso Rodriguez she spritzed on her neck and in her hair. She blinked and opened her eyes wide when I held her stare and didn't answer.

"Get out!" she said.

I rolled onto my back again and sighed.

"Bitch, are you shitting me?"

"My husband thinks I'm a heavy sleeper. I've heard him say it. *Trust me, she's a heavy sleeper.*"

Aziza sat up in the bed to better stare at me with wide eyes.

"After they'd been in the living room about twenty minutes, one time Cory stopped in the doorway of my bedroom on his way to the toilet."

"What? What did he do?"

"Nothing, he just stood there in the dark. Like he was listening, waiting for me to move or say something."

"Did you?"

"Nope. I didn't move a muscle."

"Where was Stupid?"

"I don't know, out front somewhere."

"Who is this guy again?"

"Cory. His friend Cory."

Telling Aziza about my darling husband was like waking up from a dream that I actually remembered and was able to recount in detail. Confessing my own behavior got mixed into those details until it wasn't clear anymore who was guilty and who was innocent, or if it even mattered at all.

I had a miscarriage one Friday morning after cramping on and off for hours during the night. At first I thought it was gas, or something I ate that was messing with me. When the pain moved lower, more in the belly like period pain, I knew something wasn't right. It was still early, the sun hadn't come up yet, but I got up and walked around to see if the cramping would go away. Max had gone out to a bachelor party the night before and wasn't back yet, so I didn't even bother calling him. I ended up taking a cab to the emergency room with my fingers crossed, but there wasn't much hope in my empty hands.

Clearly it wasn't a planned situation, but I had started to see having a child as a way to move into something different, something better than what I had. I was wiling to pretend my absent husband was a dream and that a child could be a new reality that I could craft and nurture on my own, if need be. Looking back, I'm glad you didn't come that way. I didn't have anything to offer yet and we would have been strangers. That's what kept me from crying as I sat in the hospital bathroom and looked down at the bloody mass in my underwear that looked like a grayish blister.

That night I was supposed to meet Aziza in Atlantic City for the weekend. She was flying up from Florida and I was going to meet her at Caesar's Palace. Our room was booked a week in advance, but neither of us made it. I sent her a message from the hospital and she hopped on a shuttle to New York. Ziz found me at home dressed in sweats, hugging a heating pad. I was only six weeks along and didn't appear to need a D&C, so the doctor had sent me home to ride it out with maxi pads and Advil. I took the pain-killers, but there was no pain. There wasn't even that much blood. There was only numbness and I didn't know what to do with it. When she arrived, Ziz dropped her bag at the door and washed her hands before crawling into bed next to me.

"Look at that, I'm wearing sweats, too."

It was a little past six in the morning and the liner framing her big eyes still looked fresh. She scanned my face, hoping for a coherent statement. I nodded and burst into tears for the first time since the whole thing happened. She gathered me in her arms and we watched the television on mute until my dear husband finally made an appearance four hours later. The fact that he had been out since the previous morning even didn't come up. On a scale of crises, my losing a baby weighed more than him being out for over twenty-four hours and strolling in like it was all fine. Ziz had tried calling his cell since she landed and never got an answer. When he showed up in the doorway there was a look of either irritation or concern on his face, but I couldn't tell which.

"Why didn't you tell me you were pregnant? Does this mean we're out of the baby business?"

Blood rushed to Aziza's face. She eased her arm from around my shoulders and turned to hide the rage radiating from her cheeks and her eyes. She got up and started gathering used tissues and empty cups. She brushed past Max without speaking on her way to the kitchen. He stepped in, closed the door behind him, and slouched at the foot of the bed. My eyes were still swollen from crying and though I had been up all night without a single thought of sleep, at that moment I thought I could drop into a coma.

He was wearing his blue suede slip-ons, pressed khakis and some designer long john top. He fiddled with a pair of sunglasses between his knees as he sat watching me take slow breaths, and long blinks. I kept telling myself that the next time I opened my eyes I would find that this was all a nightmare and I was really married to a straight man who loved me and wanted to make everything all right. He would be a man who had flaws and bad habits like laughing too loud and never picking up after himself, but he would look at me and make me feel like every part of me was sacred. I curled into a ball under the comforter and burrowed into a long blink. I opened my eyes, and the man I married was there, but the feeling I hoped for never came.

The child I lost was most likely not his. We had gone for too long without having sex for that to be possible, and we both knew it. I could confess all my transgressions. I could admit to all the men, and all the ways I gave myself away, but it wouldn't have made any difference. This man whose ring I wore looked at me with a face so blank that I didn't care anymore what he felt or didn't feel. As I lay bundled in our expensive linens, I couldn't think of anything good to say.

"How many?" I asked.

He looked up, thrown by the sound of my voice.

"How many what?"

"How many men have you been with?"

Max reached out to pat my leg like he was soothing a hurt child. His eyes shifted and he kept his tone low to keep Aziza from hearing anything.

"Olive, what are you talking about?"

"I'll take a ballpark number. How many?"

"Babe…"

"Besides Cory, I mean." Silence. "Does everyone know? Was I the last to figure the shit out?"

He pulled away with some forced incredulity twisting on his face.

"You might as well tell me the truth at this point," I insisted. "I can tell you the truth. Ask me anything. I swear I'll tell you all of it."

I couldn't muster actual anger. My words came out in sighs, too tired for fury. He sat there staring at me with his hand still on my leg. His eyes were still and empty. His face was bare except for his eyebrows and a carefully sculpted patch under his bottom lip that now looked like dirt. His mouth started moving but it was just a bunch of diplomatic double-talking about us both having made mistakes and both having failed at marriage. The more he talked about how our love had been like a piece of coal needing time and pressure to be transformed into a diamond, and some other bullshit about shooting for the moon and being among the stars, the sleepier I got. I rolled my tongue around in my mouth and realized how thirsty I was. He was still babbling vapid quotes and doing his best to look earnest, but I couldn't listen anymore. He never did respond to my accusation.

"Get out," I said, "Go back to wherever you just came from. Don't come near me again."

A week later, I was pacing the floor of the apartment, wringing my hands between fits of crying. I had left the man whose name I had taken (on paper) seven messages asking when he was going to come get the rest of his things, and still hadn't heard back. Aziza told her manager that her sister was in the hospital and took two weeks off to come camp out with me. She flew home and came back with cigarettes and tea and listened to me as I second-guessed and built myself up at the same time. While I went on with my outrage, she brewed us a concoction and sprinkled salt in it.

"What the hell is in this?"

"Ah, *habibi*, is old country secret. If I tell you, I make you disappear. You're not the only one with magic potions you know." She lounged on the sofa, letting me pace and rant a little longer while she calmly surveyed the living room. There were socks and random shoes littered across the floor. There were empty Chinese food cartons on the dining room table, some wine glasses on the TV console, and empty vodka bottles in the bathroom.

"So what are you gonna do?" She blew her cigarette smoke in the general direction of the cracked window but it still filled the room and hung above our heads for a long time before catching a soft current that pulled it outside.

"He can't even be bothered to return my calls! How screwed up can he be? I don't know how the hell I was married to this asshole."

Aziza got up and I followed her to the kitchen. She was rummaging through the cabinets until she found some heavy-duty garbage bags. I kept talking as she started picking things up and tossing them in. She didn't bother asking questions, she chose on her own what was trash and what was to keep. Cork coasters, aromatherapy diffusers, a leather briefcase, cell phone chargers, a baseball cap. She paused every now and then to take sips from her cup and nod periodically with her cigarette hanging from the side of her mouth.

"Of course his family has nothing to say. The only one who dares open his mouth at all is the father, and then it's crystal clear where this jerk gets his shit from. The rotten apple didn't fall far from the freaking rotten tree, that's for damn sure."

Aziza put her hand on my shoulder and gave me the look. She had her war paint on. Dark shadow hooded her eyes and layers of mascara made her lashes reach out like hands. It was a look that could be terrifying and mesmerizing at the same time; picture turning a corner down an ordinary block on an ordinary day and running smack into a tiger just sitting there, waiting for you. Waiting to devour you if you make another move, but beckoning you to actually come forward and step right between her jaws. I needed that look. That look was keeping me hanging on to the ledge and was willing me to climb back up.

"What am I gonna do, Ziz?"

She slid the coffee table over so that it was centered with the sofa and tossed all the *GQ* and *Men's Fitness* magazines into the garbage bag. She stood back and took a long drag of her cigarette, looked at the coffee table she had just straightened and frowned. She blew out the smoke and mashed out her cigarette on the polished surface. She looked at me and ran her fingers through her hair like she was looking in a mirror.

"Finish your tea," she said.

There were so many things for me to freak out about and I was tempted to burrow into my bed and sleep all day, but Ziz wasn't having it. One morning I woke up and found that she was sitting up next to me with a cigarette already lit.

"You know who the baddest bitch in the world is?" she asked.

"Who?"

"Scarlett O'Hara."

"From *Gone With the Wind?* The movie?"

"Yup."

"Why?"

"Think about it. Every time some shit happened to her, every time she got into some totally crazy mess, she'd say *'fiddle dee dee. I can't think about this right now. If I do I'll go crazy. I'll think about it tomorrow.'* And tomorrow just kept coming, and coming, and coming."

"And then what?"

"And that's it. Tomorrow just keeps coming. Ready or not."

I said I'd never get married again. What in the world for? What use did I have for a husband anyway? To pay my bills? To give me status? To warm my bed? I could be like Aziza, enjoying lovers on my own narrow terms and sharing my heart in rationed doses. She seemed perfectly comfortable with setting expiration dates on her relationships, even the ones that she seemed to enjoy. She left men and drew them back in as she saw fit. She'd stroke one to the point of delirium while she pushed another to the brink of a nervous breakdown. It was all a game. There was a time when I would have pitied someone who lived like that. I would have thought they were sadly scavenging scraps of the life they really wanted and settling for trying to make being single look fun. It turns out I was the one who had settled and I wasn't in a position to judge anything.

I had a dream team at the restaurant that kept the place from burning down while I was piecing myself together. My pantry cook checked in with me over the phone about setting up orders and processing the bills. I heard my hostess was cracking the whip on servers when their hair and nails weren't right. Everyone from the bartenders to the line cooks to the bussers and porters wanted to be there and it showed in their work. I took Ziz's advice and took a break. I roamed the city, took some spa days, went to the movies alone, and hung out with friends.

Divorce was definitely not a fun experience, but letting go of him was easier than I thought it would be. I separated myself from the people Max and I shared, and let myself be cocooned by those that were team me from day one. He was a dried up scab that took up space on my heart, only hanging on by a film because it didn't serve a purpose anymore on the healing flesh. I was free without him, but soon an old need started throbbing in my head like a song that always makes you cry. The melody haunts, and the lyrics are so right on that you just have to listen to it once in a while, even if it hurts. The need stretched itself out while I sat in front of the TV and watched marathons of shows I wasn't really interested in. It came along every time I was out with faceless and voiceless friends who kept watching me, hoping I didn't have a meltdown between smiles and nods. It came creeping back in softly, moaning like a ghost, rattling old shackles that I thought I had broken years before. It dragged across the floor in the middle of the night and woke me up with my heart pounding. That wretched need remembered my name and kept calling me. *Ollie,*

Ollie, oxen free... I stared up at the ceiling, asking myself if I should answer.

"Did I wake you?"

"You're lucky the shuttle was on time for once. I just got into my room. I'm having watery hot chocolate and a stale airport croissant. This shit is disgusting."

I pictured Ziz kicking off her shoes and pacing in her hotel room.

"What's up?" she asked.

"I feel weird."

"Work making you feel sick already?"

"No, I'm fine at work. The crew is tight. And thank God my fingers don't need me to tell them what to do. It's, other stuff..."

"Olive..."

"You know I'm not as hard as you."

"Thank god for that!"

"Ziz, you know what I mean."

"Where are these *bougie*-ass friends of yours? Don't they know how to look in on somebody?"

"They're not like you."

"Nobody is like me!"

"I don't think I'm as strong as I thought I was."

There was a heavy silence and I thought the line had gotten disconnected.

"Bitch, I'm alive because of how strong you are.
I just landed at Charles de Gaulle for the tenth time
in six months, enjoying the hell out of these bidets
and designer toiletries and shit at the Hilton because
of how strong you were. For me. You've got to
fight for you now."

"I'm saying I just…"

"Break something, Olive. Smash something,
whatever the fuck you have to do. But don't come
all this goddamned way just to lie down."

I used the silence to swallow down tears Ziz that
would have cursed me for.

⌘

I was browsing a farmer's market downtown in
dark glasses and a baseball cap. It was getting
warmer, but even with the bright sun, I gripped the
lapel of my coat to keep the wind from creeping in
to my chest. It was a popular spot, and people came
out in spite of the chill. Kids dragged scooters while
their moms mulled over asparagus and rhubarb. I
tapped beautiful red apples and apricots and
mushrooms. I picked up turnips and carrots that
still had earth on them, and put them back down. I
examined cute jars of raw honey, but the names
printed in charming fonts on the labels may as well

have been written in another language. I was really scanning the side streets beyond the farm fresh goods, looking for someone with a familiar strut. Someone with their hands in their pockets and their eyes quietly searching for other eyes, like mine. Without a regular number, and without wanting to pump friends for their possible regular numbers, I felt stupid checking for what I thought were familiar signs.

I picked up a jar of organic raspberry jam and walked over to the far end of the square. There was a boy wearing yellow ear-buds, holding the microphone close to his mouth and smoking a cigarette. His teeth were a little too white, his hair was styled a bit too precisely into a hip careless look. His leather jacket had an expensive designer look, but his feet confirmed that he was who I was looking for. Just below the frayed hem of his jeans, black canvas sneakers peeked out to tell me who he was. The heels were worn down on the outer edges and the white laces had turned gray. Those shoes had walked over bloodstained pavements, gutters with traces of human waste, alleys where the hip clubs has their back doors, and crowded midtown salad bars. You might not notice his shoes, if you kept staring into the mirror surface of his sunglasses. You might overlook them entirely if you lingered on his fashionable t-shirt under a blazer, or the luxury watch that hung loose around his skinny wrist.

I picked up a bag of shallots, clocking how long his phone conversation would last. I angled in the direction of the corner and saw him wave to an imaginary friend a few blocks away. He squeezed the cigarette between his lips and checked his wrist. I started toward the edge of the market holding my shallots, the jam, and a piece of goat cheese wrapped in clear plastic wrap. My hands were sweating and I adjusted my grip on the small glass jar. I stepped off the curb without looking and almost collided with a bike messenger. He whooshed past me so fast and so close that his elbow bumped my hand, making me lose my balance. I stumbled to my knees, creating a mess of shallots, jam, and glass. The cheese tumbled into the middle of the street and sat there for a few seconds before getting flattened by a Nissan. A couple of vendors rushed over to me bringing napkins and a bottle of water. They couldn't tell right away that the red goop on my hands was jam and not blood. They buzzed around me, wide-eyed and worried; someone even offered me aloe gel from one of the stalls.

The skinny guy across the street didn't see my mishap. He was still on the phone, or pretending to be. I saw him shake hands with a man in a wool V-neck. Fast, smooth, palms flat, then balled, to the pocket, exact change, done. He kept smiling, pacing, checked his watch again. Then without warning, he walked away. He disappeared down the block, getting smaller and smaller until he was gone.

"Ma'am, are you all right? She didn't get hit, did she?"

I pressed my sunglasses to my face to hide the grimace and tears that were swelling behind them.

"I'm all right. I'm all right. Thank you so much. I'm okay." I shoved a couple of twenties into someone's hand for the items I had wasted and rushed off. My hands were trembling and my glasses kept sliding down my nose.

I was still anxious when I started walking south. I had lost my baseball cap when I fell and was too embarrassed to go scrambling for it. My hair flailed and I rushed down side streets with my shoulders hunched, hoping not to run into anyone I knew. The ghosts were on my tail as I hurried past garbage cans tied to stoops with chains. A random squirrel darted out from under a car and startled me into a fit of coughing. They were quietly closing in and there was no telling how long it would take before they caught me. I had been clean for six years, but so much of my life had been prone to shattering that I started thinking that my sobriety might soon crumble, too. The ghosts were catching up, racing to drag me back to where I belonged. To wrap me in linen sheets and lay me down in a gold sarcophagus, or set me on top of a tall pyre so I could burn and float all the way up to heaven.

I cut down Bleecker, passing blocks that were grey and yawning. I kept my head down, escaping one block at a time. As I wiped my nose on my jacket sleeve, my glasses fell from my face. I accidentally stepped on them and froze looking at the plastic crumbs of my Christian Dior frames. I wasn't worried about what they cost. I just didn't want anyone to see my eyes and the panic that was growing in them block by block. I turned to my reflection in a storefront to fix my hair. The wind kept tousling it back into my eyes each time I raked it behind my ears. I came closer to the glass until I could see my hairline. The new growth had been creeping in for weeks and I worked a flat iron to keep the relaxed look going. But I wasn't relaxed at all. Tears jumped up to my eyes as I smoothed my frizz.

The glass door to my right pushed open suddenly. "Come in. There's a mirror in here."
He moved too soon for me to respond or get a good look at his face, but the growl of his voice pulled me in like a pin of light in thick darkness. I held out my hand just as the door started to swing back and I saw him disappearing down a narrow hall. I stood alone in a deceptively large space that smelled like industrial cleaner and sweat. I saw that the mirror the man mentioned actually took up an entire wall and was only interrupted by a wooden door at the end of it. The other three walls were plastered with a collage of schedules, newspaper clippings, and flyers. The counter wrapped around half the room with an old computer monitor and a roll of paper towels at the end. I walked toward my reflection, but when I got close enough I could tell that the mirror was double-sided and that there was some activity on the other side of it. I heard hitting and grunting noises and buzzers and slapping at rhythmic intervals. I squinted and made out a white mat on part of the floor and faded blue walls. There was a ring in one corner and weight machines in the other. Heavy bags hung down the middle of the room and there were speed bags on the walls. I couldn't take my eyes off the way the floor of the ring pulsed and shifted under the fighters' feet. I

leaned closer to the glass until my breath fogged against it.

The place didn't look anything like the gym I was a member at uptown. There was no bubbly blonde in a cute uniform holding a clipboard asking about your fitness goals or prior experience. No posters of models smiling against beach backgrounds flexing impossibly jacked abs and flashing veneered smiles. No air fresheners that sprayed Summer Rain at nine-minute intervals, no dance hits piping through a surround sound system. I could hear the drone of an air conditioning unit and there was a vending machine in the corner that sold water and energy drinks, but that was about it. I had my fingers pressed against the glass when he appeared again and answered my question before I came up with it.

"You can go in. Just don't get in the way." He pointed to the door and leaned back against the counter with his arms folded across his chest. I couldn't speak. Or rather, I couldn't think of anything to say that wouldn't make me sound like a mouse squeaking. His voice was gruff and low and sounded like it belonged to something with fur, heavy paws, and dangerous teeth. But his eyes were still and clear and looked at me as if he had been looking at me his whole life.

I started going by in the mornings just to sit on one of the benches and stare at whoever was in the ring. There were plenty of young guys wanting to prove that they were bad-asses. They wore sweatbands and wife beaters. They examined their bodies in the mirror as they shadowboxed for an invisible camera capturing them in all their tough glory. They hunched their shoulders and mean-mugged the heavy bag like they were going to teach it a real good lesson. They slugged hard and fast. They danced around as if to taunt the swinging bag into growing arms and hitting them back. There were balding older men with sagging guts, trying to reverse the aging process by keeping up with the bad-asses. They bought expensive gloves and wore muscle shirts. They danced and bounced, doing more bobbing and nervous weaving than actual hitting. They threw fewer punches and got tired faster, but they bragged to their friends who lived in gabardine suits and leather-soled shoes that they were "training."

Then there were the real bad-asses. The guys who could dismantle you with one punch and know that you would not be getting up after the ref had counted to ten. Or twenty. Those guys were quiet. They came in, nodded to whoever was standing at the front desk and went straight down to the locker room to get ready. They didn't waste time bullshitting about the game they watched last night or how they had to put a punk in his place at some bar. These guys changed into their shorts, laced up their shoes, wrapped their hands, and headed upstairs without a word. They warmed up with some rope then hit the bag for a while. They did the bobbing and the weaving, but it was a calculated shifting that had nothing to do with posturing and everything to do with sweet science.

The action in the ring pulled me in with every lean and shuffle. Shadows moved on the mat like ghosts chasing each other, confusing themselves with tread marks, blood smears, and sweat stains. The rhythm could be unpredictable, but it was always there. They found it while building technique, while building speed, while building power. These guys hit with an almost blank stare, their eyes stayed on target but captured all peripheral movements while checking, slipping, absorbing. When the real bad-asses danced between the ropes, they were unreadable. They paced and bounced with their lips wrapped over their mouthpieces, racing the bell. They looked smooth, ready to cut through the air like surgeons with jabs and crosses and hooks and uppercuts until the clang sent them back to their corners. I watched it all for months before I finally I put on gloves.

༄

"Hey. Did I wake you?"

"I distinctly remember sending you my schedule."

"Whatever. Can you talk?"

"I'm watching a dubbed James Bond movie. I swear, Sean Connery is even sexier in Spanish. What's up?"

"I'm fighting."

"Of course you are."

"No, I mean for real. I signed up to a boxing place downtown. It's crazy! It's all grimy and smelly and I think I'm the only girl."

"Oooh, look at you!"

"I'm terrified every time I walk in there though."

"Why? It's not like you've never bashed anyone's face open before."

"That was...."

"Another life ago. This is exercise. Training!"

"Training for what?"

"I don't know. A miracle."

"I love you."

"I know."

৵৽৽

The first time I got hit in the ring, it totally took me by surprise. I understood that gloved fists would be coming at me and I'd trained for months to prepare for that. The coach taught me about my stance, movement, maintaining distance from my opponent, and keeping my hands up to protect myself at all times. My partner was going really light since it was my first time sparring and he didn't want me to get rattled. We started out easy, getting into a groove. He tapped my shoulder and even tagged my stomach a few times, but each strike was fast and light, no pain. He was a pro who knew how not to hurt a timid first-timer. We parried a little back and forth for a while, but when he got me in the face, I froze.

Even with the thick headgear that absorbed the impact of his soft jab, I immediately lost my breath and tensed up. I circled and shifted, but I couldn't get back into a rhythm. I focused on my form and tried to keep my elbows in and my hands up by my face. I lost my stance and thought that was why I couldn't throw anything. I tried to tuck my thumbs into position in front of my knuckles but the thick leather of my gloves wouldn't let them move. The more I shuffled, the more my shoulders drooped forward and I lost my breath. My body was lean from the cardio, but I was moving like I had lead in my veins. My mouth guard was suddenly too big in my mouth and I gagged while trying to chew it into place. I could feel my hair matting under my headgear from the sweat spreading over my scalp. All the theory about the exchange of punches and strategic movement went out the window and all I could feel was the fear that had kept me paralyzed all those years ago when I was being beaten up by an opponent without gloves. My vision swam in waves, and I blacked out.

When I came to, my eyes blinked slowly trying to lock in where I was and who was talking to me.

"You OK? Hey, can you look at me? What the fuck happened to her?"

The sweat was evaporating from my skin and I became weightless. I would have floated right up to the ceiling if hands hadn't been holding me down, propped up in the corner of the ring. My partner had taken off his gloves and was loosening mine. Someone with rough hands was crouched over me wiping my mouth with some wet paper towels. Apparently, I had thrown up before passing out and made a mess all over myself and on the mat. When I tried to connect with his eyes to explain how sorry I was, he gripped my chin and gently pulled up my eyelids, turning my head left to right, patted my head and walked off. There was a damp patch near the ropes where my vomit had been and two other guys were waiting on the edge of the ring for me to get up so they could climb in. My partner handed me my gloves and helped me to my feet.

I made my way across the floor to the locker room and I imagined the bad-asses checking me out of the corner of their eyes as they jumped rope, *What the hell is this chick doing here?* As they hit the speed bag, *This ain't Lucille Roberts, honey.* As they sparred, *There's a reason you're the only girl, mama.* But no one looked at me at all. Everything continued just as it was. I couldn't tell if they thought I was pitiful or annoying or ridiculous, or if they noticed me at all.

Then suddenly the Wolf was standing between me and the stairs. He was wrapping his hands, focused on the length of fabric winding between his fingers, across his palm, around his wrist, and back again. He never took his eyes off his hands, but he was watching, taking measure of me. My hair was mangled from the headgear, my mouth tasted bitter, and my legs were still wobbly. I wondered if he could smell me from where he stood.

"Take it easy. You can try it again next week." It was the same growl that had beckoned me in on the windy day almost a year before. I had never actually seen him train in all the time I'd been going there, but the gloves he carried looked battle worn and his shoulders rippled as he wound his wraps. I couldn't tell how old he was because his body was as lean and muscled as the bad-asses, but he had long grey flecks in his wild hair that made him look even more like an animal. His eyes were clear and still, and the skin on his knuckles was thick and scarred. Every move he made held a quiet threat of devastation. He felt like a wild thing you might come upon in the woods and instead of running away, you stay, even consider getting close enough to touch because it just has to be done. With your heart pounding and with the certainty of being torn to pieces if he turned on you, you tell yourself that you must lay your hand on that fur and feel the heartbeat, no matter what happens.

He looked up at me and all of a sudden I felt like crying. I wanted someone to wipe my face and kiss my forehead and tell me that I would be okay. I wanted to be clean, to be carried to a fresh bed, and be tucked into soft sheets like a child. I swallowed the knot in my throat and tried to hide the trembling in my voice.

"I, I don't know."

"I'll be here." He tapped his glove on my shoulder as he passed me. I watched him go and tried to figure out if he meant something that he didn't say, or if he was saying something that I didn't hear. I could feel every part of myself like I had just met me there in that sweaty room. My toes crunched too tightly in my expensive boxing boots. The elastic waistband of my shorts dug into my flesh just above my belly button. My sports bra suddenly became too tight and didn't let me breathe. The veins on the backs of my hands were swollen and throbbed under the pressure of my wraps. My lips were dry but my tongue wasn't moist enough to lick them. I watched the Wolf climb into the ring and circle his opponent. It was like I had seen him do this my whole life.

DANIELLE BOURSIQUOT

8 The Promised Land

M ary Moses is here. She showed up at my door about five months after I found out you were coming. She had one of those huge black rolling suitcases and a potted plant under her arm. It had been thirteen years, and as I stood in the doorway shocked to see her tall figure filling the frame, the first thing she said to me was,

"Do you have a garden?"

"A garden?"

"I don't remember Harlem, these houses don't look like they have gardens. There has to be a place where I can plant this."

We didn't talk about the timing of her visit. Through the years our family has suffered many coincidences, many of which were never explained. Not in a way that made sense anyway.

It wasn't the first time I had lived with Mimosa. There was a ragged bush of it in the yard in Montreal, and Aunt Madeleine and Lisiane had it in their yard in Miami. Grandma Hélène had even kept a Mimosa plant in the living room of her apartment for years. I remember touching it when I was a kid, watching the little leaves close on each other like hands, then opening back up again after being left alone. She cared for that thing like it was a person, sprinkling tomato feed in the soil and keeping it evenly moist.

Mary Moses stepped in and I led her to my kitchen. I lit the flame under a full kettle and she came to stand next me as I looked into my cabinets for tea. I had everything lined up in small mason jars with neat white labels. I could feel the warmth from her shoulder to mine even though we hadn't touched yet. Without turning to look at me, she asked how many months I was. When I told her, she reached for the right jar, set it on the counter and went to sit down. I gave a quiet smile and prepared the tea she chose. Even after all these years, she didn't falter at being the Chief.

When I came to the table with the pot and two cups, she was leaning on her elbows, that same stoic face watching me move until I settled across from her and poured. We sat watching the steam rise up between us for a long time, until I thought I was being hypnotized. The house was unusually quiet because everyone had stepped out for one reason or another, leaving me alone with Mary Moses.

Without a word, she slid her hands forward. I waited for her fingers to touch mine, to take my hands to pull me in, but they stopped just short of reaching me. I waited and watched her close her eyes and lower her head onto the table. Her shoulders gave one big heave then started trembling. I was shocked because I had never seen Mary Moses prostrate, for any reason. That was not her way. By now, the anger had lifted like the steam over our tea, but the space between us was still full of echoes of old hurt. I spoke calmly, but without pause. I repeated as best as I could everything the doctor had told me.

Right about the same time he had confirmed that I was pregnant, Dr. Raymond explained that I had something called Dilated Cardiomyopathy. My heart muscles stretched and swelled trying to pump the blood my body needed until they got too weak to go on normally anymore. Even though I had been clean for almost a decade at that point, I'd made whatever this thing was worse by wearing down my heart muscle with cocaine for so long. It's funny, and kind of shitty really, that I didn't notice any real symptoms until I started improving in the ring. How about that? Just when I got a to be a badass, it kept taking me way too long to catch my breath and I was constantly tired. I dealt with it by training more and going toe to toe with some dudes in there that were like, 'Yo, man, this bitch is bad!' And then when I popped them in the mouth for calling me a bitch, they found out how bad I really was.

The doctor gave me a short list of specialists and went over treatment options, but after a while as I sat in his office, I stopped listening. He looked at me with a long pause and took my hands. Your daddy always teased and said I have man hands. When I put them up in the ring, I have to admit I did look a little mannish. I had gotten lean and my shoulders were broad and rounded. I stepped and shuffled like the guys I trained with, and I learned to hit like them, too. That day my man hands looked so small folded inside the doctor's while he talked. I closed my eyes and tried to remember my father and wondered whether this is how he would have held me before saying something scary. I squeezed my eyes shut and tried to find a tender moment with him way back somewhere in a compartment of my mind I had forgotten about. But there wasn't any.

I opened my eyes and looked at Dr. Raymond's white hair and frizzy eyebrows. Little wiry hairs peeked crazily out of his nose and for a split second I wanted to laugh at them. His veiny, speckled hands squeezed mine.

"Olive, I have to tell you that the pregnancy will put tremendous stress on your heart. Labor will do even more."

"What are you telling me?"

"Any treatment to keep you strong will involve medication that could be harmful to the fetus. And you should know that there is still time…"

"Time for what? An abortion?"

"You still have time to terminate the pregnancy safely. Yes."

Dr. Raymond let go of my hands and sat back in his chair with his palms on his knees. I couldn't stay there another second. I got up and ran out of his office swallowing air like it was water and I was dying of thirst. I stopped by the elevators and whirled around looking for the exit. Suddenly there were doors flying open everywhere and I didn't know which one to go through. They clicked and slammed making a terrible noise that had a crazy rhythm I couldn't follow. My heart was pounding and for the first time I was afraid of it. It was now a monster unfurling in the middle of me preparing for its first and only kill. I closed my eyes to stop the spinning and close all the doors. I couldn't walk through any of them yet, not until I knew what to do. I controlled my breathing the way the Wolf had taught me and I waited for the choice to come to me.

It was a blaze of hot, then a rush of cool. It was a fearsome animal growl, then a whisper of angels. Tight, then fluid. Narrow, then wide open. Dark, then light again. It was the closing of fingers one by one into a fist, then the slow release of an empty hand. The choice came to me much faster than I thought. And I did not let it go.

There was no more steam rising from our cups. The setting sun sifted through the blinds and made the whole kitchen glow. I couldn't tell if she had understood everything I'd said, she never raised her head or made any sound at all. The silence covered us both like a blanket yet my skin still crawled with goose bumps. We could have stayed in our seats, in those positions all night, without any idea of the next word that should be said. I wanted to say her name, but couldn't. Mamou was too soft and affectionate. Tante Marie Lourdes was too formal and weird since I had never even called her that anyway. Haitians can go their whole lives without ever hearing their given names out of the mouths of family members; nicknames come as a requisite with various love bonds. Finally, I slid off my stool and walked around to stand next to her. I leaned in and put my arm around her shoulders. I held her like I was holding a sleeping child, gently rocking and breathing deep.

"In my mind I always called you Mary Moses. I stopped praying when you brought me home, but that was my prayer that came true."
Her shoulders shook again, and this time I heard her muffled weeping. I rubbed her back and I didn't cry.

෨෧

Now that Uncle Aaron and the boys have gone back to Montréal and everyone else is slowly clearing out too (the Wolf's family is much bigger than mine), I come to the kitchen with you strapped to my chest and Mary Moses has breakfast and tea waiting for me. Of course she located the Haitian markets to find real peanut butter and real preserves. She bakes fresh rolls in the morning and I always has some bowl of meat seasoning for later in the day. She's rearranged our garden with a lot of the items I spend money on at fancy markets and natural food stores. Vegetables, beans, and herbs, and that Mimosa bush that sits in a corner like it's always been there watching me, hearing everything. She tells me how proud she is that I made my passion for cooking into my career. She tells me that she trusts the Wolf, and how proud she is of us.

I think about moments when your eyes will grow wide, searching for an undefined answer that I tell myself only I would have to give you. I'm gathering words like scarves and bracelets and recipes and songs to save up for those times when you'll look for me and find that I'm not where I ought to be. You certainly won't be alone. You already have a crew of cousins, with more being born as we go, so you'll have built in friends. And your daddy would face a herd of beasts to protect you. He is one. Never forget that your daddy is a wolf, and everyone is afraid of him.

But I wish you could keep sleeping against my breast and hear the sound of my heart, weak as it is, to feel safe. I wish you could keep bringing me your tears so that I can catch them and show you how to transform them into something valuable. I wish you could keep reaching for my hand, even when you're old enough not to need it anymore, but have become clever enough to sense that it's really me who still needs it.

You'll need me, and I won't be here. You'll call for me and I won't answer. There'll be longing in you that at first you won't be able to name, and when you finally understand, it will hurt. You'll cry, and you might be angry, and you might hate me for leaving you alone. I hope not.

You're not so tiny anymore. You smile and grab wiggle so much sometimes I can't stand up with you in my arms. Mary Moses looks over all the bags and boxes of gifts piling up in the parlor and shakes her head with a strange smile on her face. "You are in the garden, Olive. This is the right place to build your home."

Our yard is big enough for planting vegetables and herbs, and big enough for you to run around, when you're old enough. But that's not what she meant at all. Mary Moses talks like that sometimes, in metaphors and poetic images. She makes you have to figure out what she's telling you, instead of spelling it out directly. It can be a pain in the ass, but I think she gets it from her grandmother. My great-grandmother. Your great-great grandmother Margo.

The other day I was thinking I wanted to baptize you. When I mentioned it, everybody looked at me a little weird since I hadn't set foot in a church in so long. I think your daddy's family was Baptist at some point, but they're not so churchy either. I had something more simple in mind. As I sat at the kitchen table writing up invitations with Mary Moses, I took a look at you sleeping in your chair and I got so scared.

The fear gripped me at my throat and the more peaceful you seemed to me, the more I felt it come rolling up my mouth like vomit. Before I could control my tongue, the words came croaking out.

"Promise me you'll love her the way you love me. I want to hear you tell me that."

Mary Moses was older and time had acted on her as it does on most people. It slows you down a little. It wears you out a little and makes you less willing to bring your hand close to flames you handled with boldness before. Those flames flared up in her eyes and her hand flew up to slap my face. Her lips pursed and her eyelids twitched. Her wide hard hand stayed raised between us, cutting the air, but instead of hitting me she clamped it hard over my mouth.

In that moment I thought I saw the ghost of Margonne Impératrice appear and draw a long puff from a red pipe and blow it out like a dragon in my face. That leathery countenance with small sharp eyes hovered in smoke, and then disappeared as suddenly as it had come.

"How dare you ask me that?" It was a choked whisper. "Don't you know anything? Don't you know me by now?" she asked.

Of course I knew. But faced with the shortening of each of my breaths, I needed to be reminded. I needed for things to be branded into memory, for the repetition of truths to rise up like a wave that would wash away all doubt and carry me to the other side in peace knowing that you would be safe.

Mary Moses' love never needed a question or a prayer. It flowed like water, rough or smooth, and it never failed even when it stung like hurricane rain. Yes, I knew. There was no doubt that she would love you just as hard and just as deep as she had loved me. That kind of love never stops. It comes back. It renews itself. It's forever.

The morning of your baptism, I woke up early, even before you, and took in the way the sunlight sifts into our room. Your daddy was still asleep with his leg pressed against my hip. I sat on the bed watching you stir softly in your cradle. I put you on my chest to talk to you with my heartbeat. These are words that cannot be written or translated. These are words that exist only between you and me. When you're old enough, when you've learned enough, you'll know how to say them to someone else. But for now it's just us.

I rocked you and tickled your cheeks until your eyes opened, blinking at the light. When daddy woke up, he kissed your head and breathed in your sweet scent. We sat curled up together until we heard Mary Moses' soft knock at the door. She came in with a small wooden bowl. She uncovered it and showed me a mound of salt. We touched the bottoms of your feet with it and watched you wiggle. We each rubbed our own hands with the salt until our palms were warm and raw. Daddy cupped your head while I dipped the tip of my finger into your mouth. Your face wrinkled and contorted at first. Your little lips peeled away from my finger turning this new taste over and over on your innocent tongue. I put my finger back in your mouth and you fought the taste for a while longer. But finally you drew in my finger as normally as my breast. Every year on your birthday, put a grain of salt under your tongue to bring back this moment. Do that for me.

When you look back and try to piece together the good parts of all the stories and how they make sense, trust me everybody will have their nuggets, I realize you'll have even less of me than I had of my mother. You'll have only pictures and other people's versions, and these words. I had hoped to leave you with a lesson that will cover every issue you'll ever come across. But there are too many words and too many ways that they can be strung together to mean too many things that I know you'll learn on your own anyway.

Mary Moses told me to never make a promise. She said the price is always too high, and I could end up paying forever. You either do, or you don't do. Mary Moses, your great aunt Marie Lourdes, says that promises are full of romance, and feathers, and unrealistic expectations, and fear. I'm holding you, breathing you, salting you, and all I can say is: I promise. I promise. I promise.

9 Sugar

We did not lock eyes across a crowded room. We did not draw each other in over drinks at a bar. The first time your daddy saw me I was without my armor. I was climbing over rough hills and dragging my sword. I didn't know him when I saw him, but he knew me. He saw all the hard pieces, the hidden spring, the colors that turned like seasons over and over and over. When I was bare, he showed me how to wear fur. When my weapons had rusted, he trained me to grow claws. When I was truly hungry, he taught me the taste of flesh.

DANIELLE BOURSIQUOT

ACKNOWLEDGEMENTS

Immeasurable thanks to my editor, Lara Erhlich, who understood my vision and guided me with grace without ever meeting in person.

Fly Life Images. Pete Monsanto, for a deadbeat, you come through with amazing work.
Karama Sadaka, you gave me my cover. You made all the difference.

Patrick Anthony Howell, you've been the champion I needed at every turn. Onward.

My friends and family for their unwavering support.

Magua, who spent her life keeping my secrets.

68918950R00177

Made in the USA
Middletown, DE
18 September 2019